Legacy & Love

Paula Mowery

Published by Prism Book Group
ISBN-10: 1940099536
ISBN-13: 978-1-940099-53-8
First Edition, 2014
Published in the United States of America
Contact info: contact@prismbookgroup.com
http://www.prismbookgroup.com

THE PRAYER SHAWL

Paula Mowery

CHAPTER ONE

Sᴇᴀɴ Hᴏʟʟᴀɴᴅ Jʀ. rushed through the hospital entrance, pausing only long enough for the automatic doors to open. He shucked his jacket. The east Tennessee weather was mild for late December. This was his sister-in-law, Beth's, second trip to the maternity ward, but after today, two-year-old Miranda would be big sister to twin baby brothers. Two late Christmas presents for the whole family. His brother, Richard, had a head start in the marriage and family arena, despite being five years younger than Sean. A fact that tended to bother his mother more than it did him.

Sean stopped at the waiting room door and scanned the room. He locked eyes with his father, who waved him over.

"So, what's the status report?" Sean looked at his mother, who sat next to Beth's mother.

They spoke at the same time, glanced at each other, and laughed. Sean's mother nodded, urging Mrs. Sybrant to go ahead and give the update. "The babies are here, and everyone is doing well. We're just waiting to be able to go in." The maternal grandmother's hands fidgeted in her lap.

Sean breathed a sigh of relief, knowing everything had turned out well. There had been a possibility of complications. He plunked into a seat next to his mother and laid his arm across her shoulders. "That's great news, Granny."

Sean's mother cocked an eyebrow. "That would be Nana. Thank you very much."

All heads turned when Richard glided into the waiting room and hurried to their staked-out corner. Though his hair and clothes appeared disheveled, his face displayed a goofy smile. Mr. Holland patted his son's back. "Congratulations."

Beth's mother stood and embraced Richard. When they stepped back, the new father of twin boys ran his hand through his dark hair. "Thanks. We're ready for everyone to come in to meet Matthew and Michael."

"So, the doctor said no sign of those problems he thought would be present at birth?" Beth's mother asked.

Richard chuckled. "Nope. The doctor seemed surprised, but we told him—that's the power of prayer."

Sean suppressed the urge to roll his eyes at his brother's explanation for his healthy sons. He stayed seated, thinking two sets of grandparents was probably enough without adding an uncle into a small hospital room.

Richard glanced back. "Come on, bro, you gotta come too."

"It's not too much?"

"Naw. Beth sent me out here."

"Okay." Sean followed the eager entourage.

They gathered in a semicircle at the foot of the hospital bed. Beth lay reclined with a bundle in each arm and some sort of knitted shawl around her shoulders and draped over each baby.

A collective "ahh" emitted.

The new mother glanced to her left. "This is Matthew." Her focus moved to her right. "And, this is Michael."

Sean's mother edged nearer, fingering the soothing blue shawl draped around Michael. "Is this one of Hope's?"

A smile spread across Beth's face, and she nodded. "She brought it last week."

Beth's mother caressed the shawl's fringe that fell along Matthew's back. "Wrapped in prayer." Her voice cracked, and she sniffed.

Sean wondered about the shawl and its maker, Hope. She must be someone from their church, because he couldn't recall anyone by that name. He shook off the curiosity when the grandmothers pulled back blankets to reveal pink faces and dark hair. Sean chuckled to himself as everyone bragged about who the babies resembled. He couldn't see it.

He excused himself, giving the explanation of an early morning interview, and headed home.

As he entered his apartment, the silence was deafening after leaving the excitement of the hospital room. He opened his laptop, clicked it on, and brought up his email. Tom, a magazine publisher, asked if he had anything new. He could use a "touchy, feely" kind of story. Sean wasn't much of a "touchy, feely" kind of guy, but he'd do his best since Tom had contacted him.

HOPE WEAVER SHUCKED her scrubs and slipped into her pajamas. She grabbed an apple from the kitchen bar and as she bit into it, she checked her email. She clicked on the prayer request from her church. She smiled as she read about the safe arrival of the Holland twins.

"Thank You, God," she whispered.

Hope made a mental note to stop in for a short visit before her shift at the hospital tomorrow.

She remembered her recent shift and her time with little Hannah and her mother. She had prayed for the five-year-old girl at the request of her mother, Karen. The desperation on Karen's face clutched Hope's heart. She had prayed that if it was God's will, Hannah would be healed from her cancer. She prayed for peace and comfort.

Hope plopped into her cozy glider rocker and picked up the prayer shawl she had been crocheting for Hannah and her mother. A few more rows and then the fringe. As she moved the crochet hook in and out, shaping the stitches, Hope started to pray, just like her Mimi had taught her.

When the shawl had been thoroughly bathed in prayer, she began to hum the familiar hymn *"It is Well."* At ten-thirty, she pulled the last string of fringe through and tightened the knot. She admired her handiwork, glad she could deliver it tomorrow. A huge yawn signaled bedtime, so she folded the shawl and laid it near her purse.

SEAN JOGGED THROUGH the hospital entrance, nearly crashing into a wheelchair. He halted before making contact. "Whoa there. Sorry. I better slow myself down."

A high-pitched laugh sounded from the child being wheeled out. Sean's upbeat attitude slipped a couple of notches when he noticed the child's bald head.

As he started to stroll on by, he spotted a light blue shawl draped around the child's shoulders. It resembled the one his sister-in-law had. "That shawl," Sean said before he could reign in his words.

The slender woman walking alongside the wheelchair smiled and nodded. "Hope."

"I'm sorry. It gives you hope?"

The woman chuckled. "Well, yes, it does, but the nurse upstairs who made it. Her name is Hope."

"Ah, I see."

"It's a prayer shawl," the child said. She caressed it. "Here, feel how soft it is." Before Sean knew what was happening, the child had grabbed his hand and nudged it across the shawl. "See?"

Sean knelt eye-level with the child. "Yes, I do see."

"I'm Hannah. I'm five, and I get to go home today because of mission."

"Because of mission?" Sean glanced up at who he suspected was Hannah's mother.

She laughed and shook her head. "She means remission. Her cancer is in remission, so we're going home. Thank heavens for the shawl."

"The shawl is why you're going home?"

"Sorta. This is a prayer shawl. It represents a lot of diligent prayers lifted on Hannah's behalf." The woman patted the girl's shoulder.

Sean's mind suddenly kicked into reporter mode. "So, you say this Hope is a nurse here?"

"On the pediatric floor." Hannah's mother glanced out the door and back. "Here's our ride. Nice talking to you, Mr.?"

"Sean. Sean Holland."

Hannah waved as the wheelchair rolled toward the awaiting minivan. "Bye, Mr. Sean."

"See ya, Hannah."

Sean stood transfixed. Was this feeling in his gut the sign of a story in the making? He could certainly use the check he would get for that "touchy-feely" article for Tom. He was saving for an overseas trip somewhere. A good travel piece could give him another avenue of reporting. What could be better than traveling to some exotic location?

Sean jolted from his thoughts when the empty wheelchair whizzed past him, pushed by a tall man dressed in pale-green scrubs. Sean glanced at the gift bag in his own hand and remembered the reason he was here.

He rushed to the elevators to deliver the two teddy bears. With twin boys in the family now, there would be lots of buying double gifts.

HOPE READIED TO leave, with one last check of her reports. She smiled when she glimpsed Hannah's name. Her goal with each child remained a discharge from the hospital, even though her heart ached with the child's absence. Better well than cooped up here. She thanked God for Hannah's cancer remission. Hope was thrilled that Hannah and her mother were now believers. She had built a relationship with them over the little girl's bouts in and out of the hospital over the last year. Their time together had given her the opportunity to share Christ. Hope's Mimi had always said, "If we're open to the Lord's leading, He'll let us in on what He's doing."

Hope made her way to the maternity floor to check on Beth and the twins before she left. She knocked lightly and heard a "come in" from inside. Beth sat up in the bed, cradling one bundle while the proud daddy held the other, sitting near the head of the bed.

Both looked up and smiled—beamed might describe the expressions more fully.

"Pretty as a picture," Hope said in a low voice. "Just missing big sister."

Beth nodded. "She's with Nana and Grandpa. I'm sure she's living it up."

Richard rolled his eyes. "It'll take days of detox after being with my parents."

Hope chuckled. "Do you need anything?"

Before the couple could answer, a man breezed in. His hair was dark brown and coiffured in a short, messy, stick-up-on-top style. His baby blue eyes seemed to dance. He looked Hope up and down and then took a step back. "Oops, should I come back?"

Hope glanced at her attire. He probably thought she was the Holland's nurse. "No, I'm off duty. Just came by to check on everyone." She turned to go. "I'll let you all visit."

"Hope, wait," Beth said.

At the mention of her name, the man's head jerked around, and he stared at her. Heat rose from her neck to her cheeks under his scrutiny.

Richard stood. "This is my brother, Sean. Sean, this is Hope."

Hope recognized the resemblance. Both brothers had baby blue eyes and broad shoulders.

Sean stepped closer and studied Hope's face. It unnerved her.

"The same Hope who makes the magic shawls?"

"Excuse me?"

"You'll have to excuse him. He's a writer, a reporter—full of questions, always looking for the next story. Am I right?" Richard glanced at his wife.

Beth chuckled and nodded. "Yeah."

Hope looked Sean in the eyes and tried to keep her voice even and matter-of-fact. A warmth in her chest signaled meeting him wasn't an accident. "I do make shawls, but not magic ones. They're called prayer shawls."

There was an awkward silence as Sean held her gaze. Finally he blinked and shook his head. "Yeah, prayer shawls. I met a little girl downstairs. Hannah?"

Hope smiled at the mention of Hannah and nodded. "Little Hannah. I've prayed a lot for her."

"Obviously, Hannah and her mother think that's why she's going home and in remission."

Hope noted the sound of doubt in his tone. She straightened as tall as her petite form would allow. "God answered our prayers. He does that, you know?"

Sean diverted his gaze. "So, how are those boys?"

Hope could see from Sean's reaction that the subject of God was a sensitive one. Why? Sean's parents and Richard and Beth were believers and active at the same church Hope attended. "I'll leave you all to visit. I need to get home."

As she started toward the door, Sean's hand caught her shoulder. Their eyes met once again. "I hope I didn't offend you. It was nice to meet you."

Hope's chest fluttered, signaling her increased pulse rate, but she wasn't sure why. "Nice to meet you, too. Night."

As she left the room, heading for the parking lot, her heart raced. She opened the door of her red and white Mini-Cooper and plopped into the driver's seat. *Why did Sean Holland have such an effect on me? I'm not even sure he's a believer.*

CHAPTER TWO

SEAN ARRIVED HOME, still unable to get Nurse Hope out of his mind. She was petite with light brown hair pulled back into a ponytail. Her eyes were a tawny-green. Her mouth was small, but curved into the most pleasant smile. Hope's whole countenance exuded a compassion that calmed yet drew him. Sean was sure her patients adored her.

He rubbed his hands down his face. This was not his type of girl. With her prayer shawls and talk of God, she might just be a little too fanatical for him. But, her story could be just the "touchy-feely" angle he was looking for.

Sean could endure the religious stuff to get his story. He had long since outgrown his need for anything to do with the church or God. His family was still into that, but his college years had enlightened him to a much broader view than the narrow thinking of Christians.

Sean's mother became upset when they discussed religious beliefs, feeling she had failed him in some way since he had abandoned his Christian upbringing. He learned to steer away from such discussions, which often led to arguments and ended in his mother's tears.

Sean rolled his eyes. He couldn't help it if neither she nor his father could sufficiently answer questions he posed on the world's creation and God's supposed justice.

Besides, he was a relatively good person who obeyed the law and gave to charity. If there truly was a God who was personal and cared about Sean like he'd been taught as a boy, God would have to prove it.

HOPE RELAXED ACROSS her bed, reading her devotional passage for the day, which focused on the story of the prodigal son. As she read the last word in the scripture section, Sean's face flashed into her mind. She sat up, perplexed by the timing of the memory. Could it be that Sean was a prodigal? From his reaction to talk of prayer and God, it was a definite possibility. Could it be that God had a plan for her to help lead Sean back home?

A nudge within her spirit prompted her to begin creating another prayer shawl. Normally she knew specifically who her crocheted shawls were meant for. But, the feeling was so strong, she hurried to the living room, sat in her rocker, and began the first row, asking God's guidance.

She could almost hear her Mimi begin praying aloud. How Hope missed her. She got lost in the memory of perching on the arm of the old den chair, peering over Mimi's shoulder as the crochet needle moved rhythmically through the yarn. What would have happened to Hope if Mimi hadn't been there to take her in?

Her eyelids grew heavy until she had to lay her half-finished shawl aside and head to bed. Tomorrow was Sunday, and Hope had no shifts to cover. After Sunday school and worship, she would have plenty of time to complete the prayer shawl. Sliding into bed, she still wondered who God had in mind to be the recipient.

MONDAY MORNING HOPE folded the finished prayer shawl and placed it into her satchel along with her snack crackers, lunch, and e-reader. Upon arriving on the pediatric floor of the hospital, she stowed her belongings in her locker and proceeded to the nurses' station.

She skimmed the list of patients charged to her care. The name Grace Williams practically jumped off the screen to her attention. Hope scanned the girl's information. Grace was four years old and would be coming to the floor after her tonsils were removed and tubes were inserted into her ears.

Why had the little girl's name stood out? In all likelihood, Grace would probably not even have to spend the night, unless there was some complication. But, her spirit was piqued, ready to do whatever the Lord required.

As Hope finished her first rounds, the charge nurse alerted her to Grace's arrival. She hastened to the other end of the hall to meet her final patient. Jarod and Chris, hospital orderlies, steered the bed into room 245. A slender blonde-haired woman followed closely in behind. The woman gnawed nervously at a thumbnail.

"Ms. Williams?" Hope called to the woman.

Her head jerked toward Hope. "Yes?"

"Ms. Williams, I'm Hope. I'll be caring for Grace."

"I'm Tiffany." She wrung her hands, which trembled slightly.

Hope laid a hand on Tiffany's arm. "Everything will be fine."

Jarod and Chris exited. "Thanks, guys." She motioned Tiffany into the room in front of her. "Let me just take a look at this big girl." Hope checked her information against Grace's wristband and then began her normal vitals check.

"Is everything okay?" Tiffany's voice shook.

"Everything looks fine. Why don't you just have a seat? What can I bring you to drink?"

Tiffany eased into a chair, rubbing her upper arms. "Um, do you have something warm?"

"Sure, coffee, tea, hot chocolate."

"Hot chocolate, if it's not too much trouble." A visible shiver shook her body.

"I'll be right back." Hope sped to the lounge, mixing the hot drink and snatching the prayer shawl from her locker. Back in Grace's room, Tiffany was still sitting forward in the chair, staring at her daughter. Hope handed her the cup and draped the shawl around her shoulders.

Tiffany looked up into Hope's eyes. "What's this?"

"A prayer shawl I made. I thought it might warm and comfort you."

Tiffany's chin quivered. She set her cup on the nearby windowsill and stroked the shawl. "Did you say prayer? Are you a Christian?"

Hope nodded and knelt so she was eye-level with the woman. "Yes, I am."

Tiffany practically launched from the chair to embrace Hope. When Tiffany eased back, she adjusted the shawl back around her shoulders where it had slid slightly off. "Two weeks ago, I was saved at a women's Bible study I attended with a friend of mine."

Hope grasped her hands. "Tiffany, that is wonderful."

Tiffany glanced at Grace and then back. "I want to be a good mom." Her voice broke.

"You're on the right track. A good mom is a godly one." Hope noticed no wedding ring. "Are you single?"

Tiffany bowed her head. "Yes. My past isn't pretty."

"God takes you as you are, but he won't leave you that way. He'll mold you and lead you."

Tiffany swiped at tears from her cheeks and smiled. "Thank you."

Hope stood and patted her shoulder. "I'll be back soon."

SEAN RELAXED ON his couch, surfing the Internet. A trip and some travel writing were in his future. He needed to branch out. The articles he was writing now just didn't thrill him. Something was missing. With the approach of spring just around the corner, he could slip away for a few weeks. March was the time for spring breaks.

His cell phone buzzed. He glanced at the screen.

"Hey, Dad. What's up?"

"Son, could you come over to the house?" His tone was serious.

Sean sat up straight. "Now?"

"Please."

"I'm on my way."

Sean's heart raced, and he swiped clammy hands down his jeans. He wasn't sure what this was about, but his father's grave tone drove Sean to get to his parent's house immediately.

He gripped the steering wheel, thinking back ten years ago. His mother had just moved into the head of the department of English at the university when she was diagnosed with breast cancer. After her mastectomy, the treatments had taken such a toll on her that she had to retire. Of course, she had said God had worked everything out, because she then had the time to write and publish her Bible studies. Sean didn't think God had anything to do with it.

He pulled into his parent's driveway behind his brother's familiar minivan. He took a deep breath and bounded through the front door. He found his parents and brother in the family room. He crossed and planted a peck on his mom's forehead, then plopped down next to Richard on the couch.

"Boys, we wanted to tell you in person that Mom has breast cancer again." His father's tone was matter-of-fact. Despite that, Sean's gut wrenched.

Richard slid forward, propping his forearms on his knees. "What does that mean? Same as the last?"

"Not exactly," his mother said. "The doctor says this isn't a recurrence. It's a different type of cancer. We proceed one step at a time. I plan on having the mastectomy, then it depends on the lymph node tests as to treatments."

"When?" Sean blurted out the question before he thought. He cleared his throat. "I mean, do you have the surgery set?"

"Next week, on Tuesday." His mother's voice shook slightly. She swallowed.

"The doctor is a little more concerned this time. He wishes this had been caught sooner." The worry lines in his father's forehead were evident.

"But, we need to flood the situation with prayer. God is in control." Mother folded her hands in her lap.

Sean didn't share her confidence in prayer, but in this situation he wished he did. Before he left his parent's house, he located their church's phone directory and entered a number into his cell contact list.

As soon as he started his drive toward his apartment, he scrolled to the number and pressed call.

"Hello?" the sweet, soothing voice answered.

"Hello, yes, is this Hope? Hope Weaver, the nurse who makes the shawls?"

"Yes, this is Hope, and I do crochet prayer shawls. Who…?"

"I'm sorry, this is Sean Holland. We met a couple of months ago at the hospital. I'm Richard's brother."

"Oh, yes, I remember you."

"I hope you don't mind my call. I need to ask you a favor."

"Okay?"

"Could you make one of your prayer shawls for my mother? She has breast cancer again."

"I'm sorry to hear that. But, of course, I would be honored to do that for Mrs. Holland. She is such a godly woman."

"Um, yeah." She was right, however he didn't put much stock in all the religious stuff. But he had seen and heard people give testimony to these shawls Hope made. If there was any validity to their claims, he wanted to make sure his mother had one. "Would I need to pick it up or something?"

"Can I call you at this number? I usually deliver the shawls myself…"

"Whatever it is you do."

"I'll call you, and we can deliver it together. Okay?"

"Sure. Yeah. Thanks." Sean scratched his head. Was he completely crazy? If the shawl did nothing else, it would encourage his mother.

HOPE ENDED THE call from Sean and plopped into her glider rocker. She would've never guessed she would receive a call requesting a prayer shawl from Sean Holland. She would have never expected him to even remember her. Since she hadn't seen him in a couple of months, she had forgotten about those nudges upon meeting him. What was God up to? She reached into her crochet caddy and pulled out her needle and a soothing blue skein of yarn. Not only would each stitch be embedded with prayers for Mrs. Holland, but also for Sean.

[18]

CHAPTER THREE

HOPE COMPLETED MRS. HOLLAND's prayer shawl late Friday evening. After breakfast the next morning, she brought up Sean Holland's number and pressed send.

"Hello, Hope. You don't mind if I call you that, right?"

She stifled a giggle. "Nope, that's my name. I just wanted to let you know that your mother's shawl is complete."

"Great." There was a silent pause. "Do you…I mean, could I…?" Sean cleared his throat.

"Mr. Holland, I'm free all day if you would like to take it to your mother today."

"Sean."

"Excuse me?"

"If I'm going to call you Hope, then you have to call me Sean."

"Okay, Sean." Heat flushed her cheeks. She swallowed. "Just tell me when you want to go and give me directions to your mother's house." Hope slid a notepad over and picked up a pen.

"Oh, no, let me pick you up."

She bit her lip and sucked in a breath. "All right."

"How about around eleven?"

"That's fine." Hope rattled off her address.

The call ended, but she stared at the phone. Should she have agreed to let Sean pick her up? She gnawed her bottom lip. How was this going to look? Just the two of them showing up at his parent's house? Her stomach fluttered. She reprimanded herself. Sean didn't mean anything by this. He simply wanted the two of them to deliver the shawl together.

Hope jumped to her feet and sprinted to her bedroom. She needed something more than the comfortable clothes she had on. Finally, she settled on black slacks and a long-sleeved rose-colored blouse. She touched up her makeup and fluffed her hair. She stopped and grinned at her reflection. Why was she making such a fuss? This wasn't a date. Far from it.

SEAN PULLED INTO a space at Hope's apartment building. He sighed and shook his head. What in the world had he been thinking when he insisted on picking Hope up? Did she consider him forward? He was used to dating the women he knew. This was—what?

Movement in front of the car caught his eye. Was that Hope? The scrubs she had worn at the hospital didn't do her justice. Her black slacks and rose blouse accented her slim body. Her light brown hair hung around her shoulders, sporting blonde highlights that glinted in the sun.

Sean fumbled with his car door. He finally opened it and jumped out. "Hey, I guess you're ready."

Hope flashed a smile. Her teeth were perfect. Sean cleared his throat to cover the fact that he was staring. Mesmerized. He rushed past her to open the passenger side door. As she ducked inside, she bowed her head slightly and her lashes fluttered. His heart flip-flopped. Making his way to the driver's side, he took a deep breath and let it out. He scolded himself for his reaction.

He slid into his seat and backed the car from the spot. The silence was awkward. A question came to his mind. "How much do I owe you for the shawl?"

"Nothing. I'm just glad you asked me."

Had he offended her? His parents' house came into view. "Here we are."

Before they made it all the way up the walk, Sean's mother opened the front door, and waited in the threshold. "Hey, sweetheart." She hugged him. Sean stepped back. His mother embraced Hope.

"So good to see you, Hope. Welcome to our home." Mother motioned Hope inside.

"Thank you, Mrs. Holland."

His mother stopped in the entry and looked Hope in the eyes. "It's Rita."

Hope smiled. Mother grasped Hope's hand and led her into the family room. When everyone sat, Hope slid the shawl out of her bag and unfurled it. "Sean wanted you to have a prayer shawl for your upcoming surgery."

Mother's eyes widened, and she gazed into her son's eyes. "Thank you, son."

Hope stood. "May I?"

Mother nodded.

Hope draped the soothing blue shawl around Mothers' shoulders and then sat back down. Mother stroked the delicate fringe. Her countenance seemed to soften. "It's beautiful. Thank you, Hope."

"Could I pray for you, Rita?"

Mother's eyes were suddenly glassy, and she blinked a few times. Her lips parted momentarily but then closed. She nodded.

Hope grasped mother's hand and then reached for Sean's. When he completed the circle by gripping his mother's other hand, mother and Hope bowed their heads and closed their eyes.

Hope spoke to God as if he were right there in the room. Her words and tone were full of confidence.

Sean sensed a stirring deep inside—like someone lost now found. He shook it off. This was for his mom.

HOPE EMBRACED MRS. HOLLAND again. "You know I'll still be praying, especially next Tuesday."

"Thank you, dear."

Sean kissed his mother's cheek. Rita escorted them out and stood on her front porch as Sean jogged in front of Hope, opening the passenger side door. She turned and waved at Sean's mother and then ducked into the car.

Sean slid into the driver's side. He paused. "Do you have plans for lunch?"

Hope's breath caught. What should she say? She never expected Sean to ask her this.

He ran his fingers through his hair. "I'm sorry. You probably have things to do." He started to back from the driveway.

"Lunch sounds good."

Sean glanced her way and smiled. "Okay. What do you like?"

She shrugged. "I'm not too picky."

"Mexican?"

"Sure."

The short drive was quiet. If their meal was this silent, this would be an awkward hour. But, maybe this was God providing an opportunity for Hope to probe Sean's heart a bit.

They sat at a booth with chips and salsa between them. "Thanks again for making the shawl and going with me." His tone oozed sincerity.

"I'm truly glad you asked me, so I could pray for your mother. I have great respect for her, especially after being in one of her Bible studies last year. She's an amazing Bible teacher."

"She was an amazing English professor, too. Her students raved about her." He diverted his gaze to his tea glass, stirring the ice with his straw. "She had to give it up. The treatments from her last bout with this left her listless." His voice trailed off. He sniffed and ran a hand down his face. He looked Hope in the eyes. "People prayed then too." His tone and expression exuded deep hurt. Accusation emanated from his eyes.

Hope prayed silently for God to help her say the right things. "Your mother seemed to have ultimately come through the first surgery and treatments well."

Sean leaned his elbows on the table. "And now, she has to go through this again. Did those prayers not stick?" His question held a hint of sarcasm.

"I won't lead you to believe that I understand God's ways."

"But, why? My mother is a church attender and a good person. For goodness sake, she writes Bible studies."

"Sean, God's not punishing your mother. Things happen, but God can bring good from it. I know for a fact that your mother has testified that she was meant to retire when she first fought breast cancer."

Sean rolled his eyes and nodded. "I know, I know. She was then able to write her studies and teach them."

"Yes, and she's touched many lives."

"So, why again?" He shrugged.

"His ways aren't my ways or his thoughts my thoughts."

"What does that mean?"

Hope leaned forward. "It means I don't speak for God."

Sean's expression softened. "I just don't want her to have to go through this again. I hate it for her."

"Of course you do."

"Will you be there?"

Hope didn't know how to respond. His meaning wasn't clear.

"For the surgery. Can you be there on Tuesday?"

"Yes, I'll be there." At the moment she couldn't recall if she was scheduled to work, but she would switch if need be. Sean's pleading eyes convinced her to do whatever it took.

A smile lit Sean's face.

Their food arrived, alleviating some of the conversation's heaviness.

CHAPTER FOUR

SEAN'S REQUEST FOR Hope to be at his mom's surgery had surprised even himself. But, in his defense, she calmed and intrigued him all at the same time.

Hope was nothing like the women he went out with. Why did he even compare her with those women? This wasn't that kind of relationship. Was it?

He wasn't sure why he deemed Hope's presence necessary at the hospital on Mom's surgery day. Was he beginning to think her prayers worked? No. She did bring a positive vibe, and there was proof that a positive mindset during cancer surgeries and treatments often meant patients fared better.

Sean flipped through some more Internet travel sites, hoping to focus on something else.

Who was he trying to fool? His attraction to Hope, for lack of a better term of description, was different. Every other woman he had ever dated was shallow by comparison. Hope exuded a genuine tenderhearted compassion that pulled him in. She spoke with conviction. Even though Sean's beliefs didn't line up with hers, he had to credit her for standing on hers. He'd seen his parents frustrated when he challenged their beliefs. Hope simply stated her opinion with confidence. Sean respected that.

She was easy to look at, too. Earlier, when she emerged from her apartment building with her hair down and flashed those tawny-green eyes, he went speechless.

Even at the memory, he inhaled deep and let the air out slowly. *Stay focused.* The story of Hope and her shawls would make a great "touchy-feely" story, but that was all the involvement he needed with her.

He would write his story, get mom over this hump, and then catch a plane some place to write the next story. Maybe he would take off somewhere exotic. A date with a couple of tanned beauties would get his mind off Hope Weaver. The two of them could never work—her with a squeaky Christian witness and his knowing she was wasting her time believing lies.

HOPE CHANGED HER shift on Tuesday with ease. Her quiet times filled with fervent prayers, not only for Mrs. Holland, but for Sean. What had turned him away from God? She sipped her hot tea.

She was still surprised he had asked her to be there tomorrow during the surgery with his obvious aversion to her faith. In another situation, Hope might have been flattered to have dined with Sean Holland. She couldn't deny his attractiveness—his sculptured chin, blue eyes, broad shoulders. But the verse about not being unequally-yoked kept parading through her mind.

Why would she even think Sean would give her the time of day?

Hope rose early and packed her satchel with her Bible, e-reader, and snack crackers. She wasn't sure what to expect sitting in the waiting room with Sean. Who else might be there? She was sure Mr. Holland would be.

She kept a continual prayer line open to God, asking for His hands to be upon Mrs. Holland, and his words to be upon her lips. She entered the surgical waiting room to find Sean seated alone in one corner. His shoulders drooped. She crossed the room and stood in front of him.

"How are you doing?" She took a seat next to him. He seemed to sit up a little straighter.

"Hey. I'm okay, I guess."

Out of habit, Hope patted his knee and smiled. "Everything is going to be fine."

Sean grabbed her hand and held it. The nerves in Hope's hand stirred, and a warmth spread through her chest. Had he sensed her body's reaction to his touch? She swallowed in an attempt to calm her heart. His gaze seemed to bore deep into her.

"Thank you for being here." No words would come.

"They've taken her back now," a low voice broke in. With Sean's attention averted from her, Hope could breathe again. Mr. Holland and his son, Richard, took seats across from them. Both greeted Hope, and she returned the hellos. Her heart calmed.

She silently chided herself. She couldn't allow his good looks or his sweet gestures to get to her. Emotions were at a high today due to his mother's surgery. She wasn't here to establish that kind of relationship. Sean needed to find his way back to God, not to her.

"Would you walk with me to the cafeteria for some coffee?" Sean's question broke into her thoughts.

"Sure."

They stood.

"You guys need anything?" he asked his dad and brother.

They both shook their heads.

"We'll be right back."

Sean laid his hand gently on her lower back, guiding her out of the waiting room. *Oh, no!* There was that warm sensation again spreading up from where his hand made contact with her. Maybe she shouldn't have come.

SEAN CAUGHT HIS father and brother's eyes looking puzzled as he and Hope walked off together.

When they reached the cafeteria, she snagged a diet soda. Sean insisted on paying for both of their beverages.

The woman at the cash register smiled at Hope. "Jan, how are you?"

"I'm doing a lot better." The woman glanced at Sean and then back at Hope. "You're not working today?"

"No." Hope gestured toward Sean. "This is Sean Holland. His mother is having surgery today."

The woman nodded at Sean. "Thanks again for the shawl and the prayers."

"You're welcome"

As they walked away, Sean couldn't stop staring at Hope.

She bit her lip. "What? Do I have something on my face or something?" She rubbed the side of her mouth with her fingertips.

He chuckled. "No. You just amaze me."

She looked at the floor and a hint of pink shot to her cheeks.

He touched her arm to stop her. "I'm sorry. I didn't mean to embarrass you. It's just, I've never met anyone like you. You really do care."

She shrugged. "I can't take credit. I was raised that way."

They continued back to the waiting room. Her modesty and humility made her all the more attractive.

As soon as they took their seats across from his father and Richard, a doctor dressed in green surgical scrubs hurried over. "Rita Holland's family, right?"

His father stood. "Yes."

"We're just now getting started. There was a complication in the surgery before hers. We wanted to let you know." The man rushed off.

"Thank you." His father called after the man, plopped down again, and sighed.

Sean clenched his fists. "Great. Here I thought they might've been done or close to it." He ran his hands down his face, trying anything to remain calm.

A warm hand slid into his. Hope reached her other hand across the aisle and grasped his father's hand. They closed the circle by Dad clutching Richard's and Richard grabbing Sean's.

"God, we're frustrated." Hope's calm, sweet voice spoke. Everyone's heads bowed and eyes closed. "But, we trust you, Lord. For some reason the surgery needed to begin later. Guide the surgeon's hands. Draw near to my sister, Rita. And comfort us as we await word. In Jesus' name, amen."

His father patted Hope's hand. "Thank you." His voice was low and shaky.

Sean needed to lighten the moment and focus on something else.

"Hope, how did you start making the shawls?"

He sounded like a reporter, but diverting attention from the surgery called for quick thinking.

Hope folded her legs under her. "I have my Mimi to thank for that. She was my mom's mother." She shook her head and smiled. "As a girl I would sit on the arm of her chair, looking over her shoulder as she crocheted. What a prayer warrior! Even as a youngster I can remember the goose bumps crawling up my arms listening to her petition God on behalf of a sick brother or sister in Christ." Hope's chin quivered. "I miss her. She not only taught me to make the prayer shawls, but she's the reason I became a nurse. For years, Mimi would sit and care for sick people in their homes. Most of them until they passed on to glory."

His father leaned forward. "I remember your Mimi. She sat with my grandmother. I can remember stopping in to visit and hearing her singing 'It is Well.' I'll never forget it."

Sean was an outsider. Their strong beliefs seemed to connect them, bind them together like a family. Even though he was here with his own father and brother, his biologically connected family, Sean lacked their camaraderie.

Sean listened as the three conversed about church happenings and people they held in common.

He spotted the surgeon and stood, hoping the operation was completed. When the doctor neared, everyone else stood.

"Mrs. Holland's surgery went well. I think we got it all. We'll test the lymph nodes we removed, of course. Since it's later, I'm going to keep her overnight."

"Thank you. I'll be staying with her," his father said. "Where should I go?"

"She'll be in recovery a bit longer, but then she'll go up to the second floor. I think she's already been assigned a room. Ask at the nurse's desk there." The doctor turned and rushed out.

Arms pulled Sean into a group embrace. When they stepped back, his father sniffed and picked up his duffle. "I'll go on up and wait for her to get to the room." He turned to Richard. "You go home and check on your family." He focused on Sean and Hope.

"Dad, you probably need to eat," Sean said.

"I don't want to leave. I need to be there when she gets to the room. You two go on. You need to eat, too."

Sean ran his hand through his hair. "We'll go grab something and bring something back for you. Okay?"

"Agreed."

They walked to the hallway, seeing his father onto the elevator. Sean turned to his brother. "Do you want to go eat with us? You probably need something, too."

"Naw, y'all go ahead. I better go check on my gang. I might need to run out for a bite for us. Give my tired wife a break. Just make sure to bring Dad something."

"Okay."

"Thanks, Hope." His brother patted Hope's shoulder.

CHAPTER FIVE

THEY STEPPED OUTSIDE. A light rain fell.

"You wait here. I'll pick you up." Sean jogged off before Hope could protest, which he was sure she would do.

He pulled to the curb and Hope slid in. "Thanks. You didn't have to do that. I won't melt."

"I don't know about that."

Their eyes met, and she quickly diverted her gaze to her lap.

After a quick discussion, they ended up at a local steak house.

"I think everything looks good for your mother." Hope smoothed the napkin across her legs and flashed a smile.

"Yeah, so far. It was those terrible treatments that got her the last time." As he watched Hope sip her diet soda, he wondered if she had so easily kept her faith due to her easy life. Except for losing her grandmother, Hope had never mentioned true hardship. Maybe that was why her belief in God stayed intact. She'd never had it tested.

"What are you thinking?" Her eyes stared into his as if trying to read his mind. "Your mother is in good hands."

"I know. That surgeon is one of the best…"

"That wasn't the hands I was referring to." Her brows arched.

"About that, can I be honest?" He swiped his hand down his face.

"Of course."

"I'm thinking you've never had a reason to lose your faith in your God."

Hope licked her lips and leaned forward. "Well, you would be wrong."

Sean rested his forearms on the table. "I mean, I know you lost your Mimi, and I'm sure that was hard. You were obviously pretty close to her, but…"

"Yes, I was very close to her." She paused and sighed. "Especially due to the fact that I had to move in with her during high school, after my parents were killed in a car accident."

Sean winced. He instantly regretted voicing his assumption. "Hope, I'm sorry."

"No, it's okay." She sipped her drink and then trained her eyes on his. "I can't lie to you. My faith wavered. I couldn't understand why a sixteen year old would lose both her parents. I still don't, but God took care of me." She lowered her gaze.

"What? What are you thinking?" Sean wondered at her pensive expression.

"I couldn't have made it this far through so many losses without God being with me." She bit her bottom lip.

"Do you have any other family?"

She shook her head slowly. "I was engaged once."

Sean sat up straight. "That guy must have been crazy to let you get away."

"Well, he didn't really have a choice."

"Oh? You broke his heart?"

"No. Travis was a firefighter. We met one night when I filled in down in Emergency. We dated six months, and he proposed. The wedding was set for October 21st, but in September there was a house fire. He saved a little boy, but…Travis' injuries were fatal."

Sean's chest tightened. He stroked his chin. "I'm sorry." Nothing more came to mind. He had no idea Hope's life had been so tumultuous. Sean only respected her more knowing her painful past. Whether he agreed with her faith in God or not, her life experiences would make a good story. Someone might be encouraged by her. This was much more than just a 'touchy-feely' article to get a paycheck. "Hope, could I ask a favor?"

Her brows rose. "Sure."

"Will you allow me to write an article about you for a magazine?"

She laid her hand on her chest. "Me?"

"Yeah. I want to tell a little about your past and about the prayer shawls. I think it might encourage people."

"Well, I…"

"I promise to let you okay everything." This was just the story the publisher had been wanting. "What do you say?"

She shrugged one shoulder. "I guess."

He reached his hand across the table, laying it on top of hers. "It'll be great. Of course, it means you may have to put up with a few more dinners and a little more interviewing."

She grinned. "Okay."

Sean was glad she agreed to the article. But, was he more pleased that he had an excuse to see her again?

HOPE LAY IN her bed, staring at the ceiling. So that was Sean's angle. He wanted to write an article. He seemed sincere that this story would encourage others. Was that just his tactic to convince her?

She sighed and flipped to her side. Either way, he would have to hear about her faith. That was the point, right? To bring Sean back to the Father?

The Lord would have to help her with her emotions. Sean looked at this situation as an assignment, and she should too.

After her shift the next day, she checked her phone, and it indicated she had a new text message. It was Sean. Her stomach fluttered slightly. She rolled her eyes at the reaction. He inquired about her plans for Friday night. She hit reply and typed back, "No plans."

His answer came immediately. "Italian. Pick you up around six."

She typed out an "okay" not adding the "sounds good" though she thought it.

Hope gnawed at her bottom lip and tried with all her might to suppress the anticipation. If she didn't calm her attraction to this man, she was sure she was headed for embarrassment and hurt.

CHAPTER SIX

SEAN EMAILED TOM about the article on Hope and her prayer shawls, and the magazine publisher was intrigued. Sean promised to have the completed story in two weeks. He just needed a little more information to finish.

His phone buzzed, and he glanced at the screen. "Mom, hey. How are you feeling?"

"I'm feeling especially great after talking to the doctor." Her exuberance bubbled through a giggle.

"Oh?"

"The lymph nodes were clear, and I won't require any treatments at all. Isn't that great?"

"Oh, Mom, that's more than great. I can't wait to tell Hope."

"Hope?"

"Yeah, I'm taking her out for Italian tonight."

"Really?" Her voice lilted.

"Mom, I'm interviewing her for a magazine story."

"Okay, well, tell her I said hello." Her tone hinted at not believing his motives for taking Hope out.

Mom knew better than to consider the two of them a couple. But, he couldn't deny his eagerness about having dinner with Hope again.

HOPE ADMIRED SEAN'S strong profile as he gave their order to the waitress.

They had decided to split a large entrée in hopes of having dessert, which appealed to her particular love for cheesecake.

She plunked a breadstick onto a small plate and instinctively bowed her head and closed her eyes. She paused and peeked at Sean.

He waved his hand dismissively. "Go ahead."

She closed her eyes and prayed silently. When she raised her head, she couldn't help probing Sean a bit. "I'm curious. Your family are faithful church attenders and strong Christians."

"Well, yeah." He shrugged.

"So, how come you're not?"

"I grew up in it all—going to church, involved in various groups. I had this friend named Ben. We got pretty tight in the youth group at church. When we graduated from high school, we went to a local Bible college. We were roommates. One night he came back to our dorm room drunk. I was afraid someone would find out, especially when he kept getting sick in his bed. The problem was if he got caught, I would be kicked out as well."

"That doesn't seem fair."

"No, but that was the rule. So, I pulled him out of bed and stuck him in the shower while I changed his sheets. I finally got him back to bed, but the next morning I overheard him make fun of what I had done to some other guys."

"That stinks."

"Yeah, it did, but Ben went on as if he were the perfect Christian. I couldn't stand the hypocrisy, so I transferred to another college. The professors there helped me to see that I was following a ruse."

"In what way?"

"All of that Christian doctrine shoved down kids' throats to mold them into what parents want and believe. I finally started thinking for myself."

He sat up a little straighter. His fall from faith in God sounded like the perfect storm. Hope wanted to probe deeper, but Sean quickly continued on. "But, I didn't come to talk about me. I have some questions for the article."

THE REST OF the dinner conversation never reverted back to Sean. Hope was glad to have gained some insight into Sean's adverse feelings toward God. They finished and headed toward her apartment.

Sean pulled into a parking space, jumped out, and opened her door in a most gentlemanly manner. Why did he have to spurn God? This could all work out much differently if he just believed the way she did. It wasn't meant to be.

"Thank you for dinner and dessert." She giggled.

"You're welcome. Thanks for the story."

"I can't imagine that anyone would be interested in reading about plain ol' me."

"Nonsense." He drew closer and gazed into her eyes.

Hope's stomach tightened. He leaned his head closer. What was he doing?

The warmth of his breath caressed her chin. Before she could process his nearness, he brushed her lips with a kiss. Her pulse pounded and her whole body tingled.

Sean studied her face and stepped back. "I'm sorry."

Hope shook her head and diverted her gaze to the ground. Her heart would surely leap from her chest if she didn't avoid his eyes for a moment. She swallowed hard and eased her head up, meeting his probing gaze.

"I'll see you around. I better go home and finish this article before I get myself in trouble. I'll email you a copy before I send it, okay?"

"Okay."

He pressed his lips tight and sighed, then he jogged around to the driver's side and hopped in.

Hope waved to him as he drove away. Finally, she started breathing again. She fairly floated to her door and fumbled with her key. She made it inside and plopped onto the couch. What did he mean when he said he should leave before he got in trouble? Could he have possibly experienced a reaction when he kissed her? Hope slammed her body against the back of the couch and slouched. She puffed out her cheeks and let the air out slowly.

Sean had apologized for the kiss. Maybe that was just something he did naturally, and she had acted like some love-struck teen.

She would snap out of this. The article was almost finished, and he would move on to his next subject.

Hope sat up straight on the edge of the sofa. She needed to move on too, out of this hint of fantasy she had allowed, and back to real life.

SEAN SAT IN his home office and struggled to finish the article on Hope without his mind wandering.

He had kissed her before he could reign himself in. He could have sworn she reacted favorably too, but her true feelings were

[39]

masked by the look of shock on her face. He needed to back off. The two of them had too many differences to try for any kind of relationship, though he wished the situation was different.

He adjusted his chair and put his fingers back on the laptop keys, determined to be done with this assignment. He had narrowed down his trip to a couple of destinations. When he nailed down the specifics, he was off to attempt his hand at travel writing.

Mom was out of the woods. Everything was perfect for a new endeavor.

CHAPTER SEVEN

SEAN'S CELL PHONE buzzed.

"Tom? I hope the article was to your liking. You don't normally call me personally."

"Sean, my man, this article was perfect. I actually built a lot of the June theme around it."

"I don't know about perfect, but I'm glad it worked out so well."

"Listen, I've called to offer you an ongoing gig. How about spiritual perspectives by Sean Holland Jr.?"

Sean winced. Tom had to be kidding.

"Sean, you still there?"

"Yeah, man. You kinda surprised me with this one."

"Well, what do you say?"

"Tom, I don't know. I'm not sure I could do a spiritual-type column justice."

"Nonsense."

"Look, I'm actually getting ready to take a trip to Italy. Try my hand at travel writing."

"Oh."

"I'm sorry, man."

"Well…if you change your mind, you know how to find me."

"Thanks, I'll keep that in mind."

As Sean ended the call, he eased into a nearby chair. He rubbed his hands down his face. An offer from Tom for an ongoing column was big, but he couldn't continue to write about things he didn't believe in. He shook his head. He hadn't expected something like this to come of the article about Hope and her prayer shawls.

Sean had a plan for his Italy trip. All he had to do now was secure his airline ticket and book the accommodations he found on the Internet.

His phone buzzed. Glancing at the screen, he didn't recognize the name, but decided to answer anyway.

"Sean Holland?"

"Mr. Holland, my name is Andee Collins. I'm a lawyer handling the last will and testament of Ms. Tiffany Williams."

Sean scanned his memory. A picture of the beautiful blonde flashed across his mind. But, wait, last will and testament?

"Did you say will? Has Tiffany…?"

"Yes, sir. Ms. Williams was killed in a car accident. Could you come to my office? I need to inform you of some provisions regarding you."

Why would Tiffany name him in her will? The two of them had dated only about six months. That had been five, maybe six years ago.

"I was just about to do some errands. Could I stop by now? Are you available?"

"That will be just fine."

After giving Sean directions to her office, the lawyer hung up. Sean was glad she could see him now, or his curiosity might have eaten him alive. He parked in front of the simple brick building and entered the small lobby area. A white-haired woman looked up from the papers on her desk and raised her eyebrows. "May I help you?"

"I'm Sean Holland. I'm here to see Mrs. Collins."

"She's expecting you." The woman stood. "This way."

Sean followed her to the end of a small hallway, which opened into a conference room. The brunette behind the table stood and extended her hand.

"Mr. Holland, I'm Mrs. Collins. Please have a seat."

As Sean sat he felt a little like he was at the principal's office. His stomach turned queasy. Mrs. Collins opened a folder and began to read.

"I, Tiffany Williams, being of sound body and mind do appoint Sean Holland as legal guardian over our daughter, Grace Williams, upon my death. He will assume immediate custody."

The sick feeling in Sean's stomach increased, and a dizzying fog settled around him. With an emphatic shake of his head, he struggled to clear his thoughts. Mrs. Collins eyed him, obviously awaiting a reply.

Words formed but were jumbled. A daughter. Custody. Mistake.

"There must be some mistake," Sean finally forced out.

"I take it from your reaction that you were unaware of this guardianship?"

"Unaware of a daughter." His voice squeaked at a high pitch.

The lawyer's eyes widened. "I see. But, this has all been spelled out specifically and legally." She shuffled through the folder. "The child's grandmother is on her way here with Grace."

"Why doesn't her grandmother keep her? I mean, I don't even know the kid." Sean struggled to breath.

"The guardianship is designated as you, Mr. Holland."

A commotion in the lobby caught the lawyer's attention.

"Will you excuse me?"

Sean nodded. He ran his fingers through his hair and sighed.

"Mr. Holland?"

Sean jumped at the address. He stood. "Yes?' He moved to the conference room threshold. A small, white-haired woman sat on a powered wheelchair. She was forced to remain in the hallway for there was not enough space for her to enter the room.

The woman narrowed her eyes and gazed at Sean. "You are Sean Holland?"

"Yes, ma'am." His mouth went dry.

"I'm Mrs. Williams."

Silence ensued. A little hand grasped the side of the woman's chair and a blonde head peeked from behind. The child's gray-blue eyes met Sean's. He stifled a gasp. No need for any tests. Grace looked just like him.

Mrs. Williams glanced over her shoulder. "Come here, child." Her voice was gruff. "This is Grace. Her things are in the lobby."

Grace's little body trembled. Sean's heart cinched. This mess wasn't her fault, and she was obviously petrified. Sean knelt on one knee. "Hey, Grace, how old are you?"

She held up one pudgy hand.

"Five?"

She nodded vigorously.

Her grandmother flicked her controls, twirling the wheeled chair around. She disappeared down the hallway without a word. The little girl's chin quivered.

Mrs. Collin's voice echoed in the background. "Mrs. Williams is the only known relative. A widow with disabilities."

Was it possible that Sean was actually the better choice for Grace? The only problem with that scenario was he had no idea how to take care of a child.

"Her mother wrote you a note." The lawyer thrust an envelope into Sean's hand. Her expression let him know the meeting was over.

As he eased toward the door, Grace reached her hand his way. He took it and allowed her to lead him to the lobby. She plopped on the floor and opened a pink suitcase, pulling out a worn teddy bear.

Sean sank into a nearby chair and pulled out the letter. He scanned it silently.

Dear Sean,

If you are reading this, then something has happened to me, leaving Grace alone.

The only other alternative is my mother, but she is really not able to care for Grace. I started to call or write to tell you about our daughter so many times, but I just couldn't, since we didn't part on very good terms. As you might have noticed, she looks so much like you. She is so precious, and I only want what's best for her. Please care for her despite your feelings for me.

Tiffany Williams

Sean folded the letter and stuck it back into the envelope.

"Mr. Holland, I need to give you some more information about monies set aside for Grace," Mrs. Collins said.

Sean glanced at Grace, who was still clutching the worn brown teddy bear under her chin. He extended his hand toward her. She eyed it a moment and then placed her little hand in his. They followed the lawyer back to the conference room. After another half hour of legal mumbo-jumbo, he loaded Grace and her two small bags into his car. The challenge was attaching the booster-type car

[45]

seat into the car's back seat. He finally had Grace strapped in. Now what?

"Are you hungry?" He looked at her in his rearview mirror and her little head bobbed up and down.

Where did five year olds eat? He re-gripped the steering wheel a little tighter.

"Can we have chicken nuggets?" Grace's small high-pitched voice broke into his thoughts.

"You mean like from McDonalds?"

He watched as her head bobbed again. That was probably a good idea. He could grab the fast food and head home. He wasn't quite ready to run into someone he knew and be required to explain about Grace. What would he say? This situation was surreal. He pulled through the drive through and ordered their meals. He retrieved the food and headed to his condo.

"Mommy doesn't usually let me have soda. But, sometimes for special 'casions."

Sean hadn't thought about that. "It'll be okay. It's just a small drink."

"Okay."

Arriving at his building, he had to make two trips to get the food and suitcases inside. He opened Grace's meal and placed it on his dining table. She struggled into the chair, needing a boost. When she sat down, her eyes were level with the table's edge. That wasn't going to work.

"Tell ya what. How about we go into the living room and use the coffee table?"

Grace shrugged. He lifted her from the chair and set her on the floor. He grabbed her food and headed for the lower table. He swiped several magazines to the side.

"Now, try that."

"Mommy doesn't let me eat in the living room, 'cause I might spill."

"It's okay. Your drink has a lid."

That seemed to satisfy her, because she dove into the chicken nuggets and fries as if she hadn't eaten for a week.

How would he explain this to his parents? What was he going to do with her while he worked? Work. Thank goodness he hadn't purchased any tickets for his trip to Italy. How could this be happening right now? There had to be something he could do. He couldn't raise this child. He wasn't sure he wanted to. Maybe Tiffany's mother wouldn't be all that bad. But, if Tiffany had actually chosen him over her mother, then there had to be some issues there. He ran his fingers through his hair.

Movement caught his eye. Grace stood fidgeting.

"I need to go potty."

"Okay."

"I can go all by myself."

Relief rushed over him. He sprinted to the bathroom door, ushering her in. He returned to his seat in the living room. The toilet flushed, and Grace sauntered into the room, struggling with her pants. She stopped and huffed.

"I can't get these things snapped."

"Oh, here, let me try."

Sean fumbled with the fastener until he finally heard the snap close.

"Thank you." She flashed a grin.

"You're welcome."

Grace crossed her arms across her chest. "My Grammy said that you're my daddy." Her little gray-blue eyes stared into Sean's.

He cleared his throat. "Well, yes, it would seem your Grammy was right."

CHAPTER EIGHT

HOPE READ THE article again. Sean was truly a gifted writer. She still couldn't believe the subject of the story was her, and this magazine was read all across the country. Several of the nurses and doctors at the hospital today had commented on the article. She had debated all day about calling Sean to thank him and compliment his writing. But, would that be disastrous? No, she was just being courteous and showing her gratitude. She punched Sean's number and her stomach fluttered at the first ring.

"Hope, how are you?"

"I'm doing really well and you?"

"Good too."

"I just had to call…" A commotion stopped Hope.

"I'm sorry. Could you hold on a moment?"

"Sure."

Sean's muffled voice came across the phone. She cupped her forehead. He wasn't alone. How embarrassing. Stay in control. She had called for a reason.

"Sorry."

"That's all right. I don't mean to interrupt. I just wanted to thank you for the article. It was nicely done."

"I'm so glad you're pleased. Listen, I hate to go so quickly, but I'm a little tied up."

"Oh, yeah, sure."

Hope slouched in her glider rocker. Why had she called? Now she felt foolish. Sean obviously had company of the female persuasion. Why was she so shocked? It had been a couple of months. She picked up her latest crochet shawl project. *Just forget about him.*

SEAN HATED TO cut Hope off with such haste, but he was trying to get Grace settled into the guest room. He had considered contacting Hope over the last few months but had never brought himself to do it, and he wasn't ready to admit this new development to Hope either. She would truly think he was a heathen now.

Grace's eyes drooped, and she rubbed them with her fists.

"Here, I'll help you onto the bed." He deposited her right in the middle. "It's a little high."

Her mouth opened in a huge yawn. "I need my jammies."

"Where are they?"

She pointed. "Pink bag."

Sean knelt and unzipped the small suitcase. He glanced back at Grace. "What do they look like?"

"Purple with a princess on it."

He moved folded garments until he spotted something purple. When he pulled the pajamas out, something else came out. His breath caught in his throat. A soft blue shawl. It had to be one of Hope's. But, how...? He stood. "Grace, what is this?"

Grace's face lit with a sleepy grin. "That's a prayer shawl."

"Where did you get it?"

"From the nurse at the hospital when I had my tonsils out."

Grace struggled with getting her shirt over her head. Sean set the shawl aside and helped as best as he could. By the time she cuddled her bear and laid her head on the pillow, she was asleep. Her face was angelic with the bedside lamp's glow radiating from her cheeks.

He tiptoed back to the living room and plopped onto the couch with a sigh.

What a day! There was a lot to work out. And, how ironic to discover one of Hope's prayer shawls. His eyelids were suddenly heavy. He would just stretch out here for a few minutes.

He jolted awake. Wailing sobs came from the guest room. He jumped to his feet, and his head swam momentarily. Finally steady, he sprinted down the short hall.

Grace sat cross-legged, rocking back and forth. Sean could now make out her words. She was calling out for her mommy. Each sob pricked his heart. His chest tightened. He slid onto the bed next to her and slipped an arm around her little shoulders. She leaned into him and scooted closer. Her body shook, and many sobs came out in hiccups. He had to calm her. Sean pulled her onto his lap, and she laid her head on his chest. Her arms wrapped around his sides. He returned the embrace and rubbed her back.

Her crying calmed, and then her shoulders slumped. She was finally back to sleep. He tried to move her from his lap and lay her again on the pillow, but she startled awake. Sean pulled her close again. Her breathing evened out. Finally, he just eased back, letting her settle onto his chest.

Sean woke to find Grace on her knees at his side, staring at him.

"Are you awake?" Her question was voiced with a whining tone.

He rubbed a hand down his face. "I think so."

She propped her elbows on his ribs and leaned her chin on her fists. "Are you hungry?"

Sean stifled a laugh. "Yep, I believe I am. What do you like to eat for breakfast?"

"Well, I think I want peanut butter toast. Do you like that? I can show you how to make it." Her eyes widened.

"Okay." He sat up.

Grace shimmied off the bed. "Come on." She extended her hand, palm up and flipped her fingers back-and-forth in a "follow me" gesture.

Sean chuckled and followed her to the kitchen. This kid could certainly be irresistibly cute.

How could he raise a child? Where would Grace fit into his life? Then again, where could Grace go? He had always been independent, never tied down, able to go and to do whatever he wanted when the whim hit him. He needed help.

CHAPTER NINE

HOPE TRUDGED THROUGH her apartment door after working a longer shift than expected. She flopped onto the couch, putting her tired feet up. A muffled buzz sounded from her purse. Her phone. Could it wait? She hesitated. No, she should check it. She dashed to the table and fished out the still buzzing cell. She stared at the screen. Sean Holland.

"Sean? Hey, this is Hope."

Screams almost covered Sean's reply. "I need help. Can you please come to my condo?"

What was going on? By the desperate tone in his voice, something was really wrong. And, that screaming and wailing in the background sounded like a child.

"Sure. What do…?"

"I'll explain when you get here. I'm really in over my head."

"Okay. I'll change and be right over".

"Thank you."

As she knocked on Sean's door fifteen minutes later, cries still echoed from inside. As the door opened, Sean uttered a thank goodness and grabbed her hand, pulling her inside. His eyes were bloodshot, and his overall appearance could only be described as disheveled. Not at all the Sean Holland she had come to know. He closed the door behind her, and it was then she spotted the source of the crying.

A small girl sat on the couch rocking a stuffed bear with one of Hope's prayer shawls draped around her shoulders. Tears streamed down the little girl's cheeks, and her sobs came out as hiccups. Hope glanced at Sean, unable to speak. He ushered her closer to the child.

"This is Grace Williams. My daughter." He leaned close to her ear. "I didn't know about her until I was contacted by a lawyer. Her mother was killed in an accident. Her will named me as guardian."

Hope's heart wrenched. She gestured toward Grace. "The shawl?"

"It was in her suitcase. It's one of yours, isn't it?" His eyes widened.

She nodded. Focusing on the child, she eased near and knelt in front of her. "Grace?"

The girl's eyes gazed into Hope's. Her face was covered with dark pink blotches, and her eyes were red rimmed. Tears had made her eyelashes clump. Suddenly recognition dawned in Hope's mind.

She glanced at Sean. "I remember. Several months ago around January, Grace had her tonsils out.

"And tubes in my ears," Grace added, sitting up a bit straighter.

Hope turned back toward her. "That's right, sweetie."

Grace studied Hope's face for a moment, and then her eyes bulged, and her mouth fell open. "You took care of me and gave my mommy this shawl." She stroked the fringe.

"Yes."

Grace launched herself into Hope's arms and nearly landed them both on the coffee table. Hope righted them, wrapped her arms around the child, and returned the tight embrace.

Hope locked her eyes on Sean, who plopped down on the couch and sighed. "I knew if anyone could help, it would be you."

Grace went limp in Hope's arms, and her breathing evened. "I think she has exhausted herself from crying."

Sean scrubbed his hands down his face. "What am I going to do? I don't know anything about taking care of a child." He scooted to the edge of the couch. "Is there somewhere for her to go? You know, where she can be better cared for?"

Grace fidgeted. Hope stroked her hair, and she quieted again. "Sean, you're her father. Do you really want to throw her into foster care? You can't be sure who she'll end up with, and she may be moved from place to place. That's traumatic, especially for such a young child."

"Sounds like you know this from experience."

Her eyes stung. She blinked to stave off the tears. Sean probably didn't need another crying female. "I do know from experience. When my parents were killed, my living with Mimi wasn't immediate. I bounced around from foster home to foster home for almost five months before my Mimi could get everything squared away. My parents hadn't thought ahead like Tiffany did."

"Hope, I'm sorry."

She shook her head. "Sean, you can do this."

"How?" His voice rose. He paused and lightened his tone. "How do I do this?"

An urging bubbled from deep inside Hope. "I'll help you." She blurted out the words before she could stop herself. "She was here last night when I called, wasn't she?"

Sean nodded. "She went right to sleep but woke up screaming in the middle of the night."

"What did you do?"

"I rushed in, and she pretty much did what she has with you. When I tried to lay her down to leave, she almost woke again, so I just laid down with her on my chest."

Hope smiled. "See, you're not as bad at this as you think."

"I'm still in shock. I never knew about her."

Hope smoothed Grace's hair and studied the side of her face. "She looks like you."

"I know." He smiled.

HOPE AWOKE STRETCHED out on Sean's couch, Grace wedged between the sofa back and Hope's side. She barely remembered moving from the floor. Light shone in rays around the long, slatted blinds on the sliding-glass door. Grace had slept through the night. Hope winced at the thought that she had spent the night in a man's condo. Sean Holland's, no less. But, it had been more like a sleepover with Grace. After she saw the desperation in his eyes, she couldn't leave him. Sean had practically begged her for help.

Hope's hair was grimy, and she longed to rush home for a shower and a change of clothes, especially before Sean saw her. She was stuck. She feared moving, which surely would awaken Grace. Today was Saturday. No shifts to work today or tomorrow.

Light footsteps caught her attention. Sean appeared from around the corner that led to the hall. He stopped and stared down at her. "Did she sleep all night through? I didn't hear her," he whispered.

Hope nodded. "Yes."

Sean lowered himself and perched on the edge of the coffee table. "Do you have to work today?"

"No. I don't have another shift until Monday."

Grace suddenly stirred and sat up, rubbing her eyes with her fists. "I need to go potty." Hope swung her feet to the floor, sitting up. The girl hopped down and scampered off.

Hope turned back to find Sean looking at her. She smoothed her hair and stuck it behind her ears. "I better get home and take a shower." She stood, scanning the area for her purse.

Sean shot to his feet. "You'll come back, won't you?" At that moment he resembled a scared little boy.

"Yes, I'll come back." She nodded.

"What should I do while you're gone?"

Poor man. He really was quite lost in this situation.

"Tell you what. You and Grace unpack her suitcases and find a place for all her things. Notice what she has. We'll talk about it when I return."

"Okay."

Grace stood at the living room entrance. "Are you leaving?" Her bottom lip protruded.

Hope closed the distance between them and knelt to the little girl's level. "I have to run home to get a shower and change clothes." She glanced at Sean and then back. "While I'm gone, you two get your bags unpacked. I'll bring back a couple of surprises. Does that sound good?"

Grace nodded her head vigorously

Hope stood and grabbed her purse. "I'll bring late lunch/early supper, okay?"

Sean nodded.

Hope stifled a chuckle. There was no denying that the two were father and daughter. Their similarities screamed.

CHAPTER TEN

SEAN FEARED UNPACKING Grace's suitcases would not fill enough time, but the task lasted almost two hours. Grace chattered about each item she withdrew from her bags. Sean had no idea that such an oratorio could be given on socks and their precise placing in the chest of drawers. When the unpacking was complete and her suitcases stowed in the bottom of her chest, another forty minutes passed as she picked an outfit for the day. As she pulled on her last sock, the doorbell rang. Sean rushed to the door and opened it to find Hope, her arms filled with loaded plastic grocery bags.

"Here, let me help you." He relieved her of two bags and led her to the kitchen. She dropped her parcels on the counter and sighed. Sean peered into one of the bags. "What is all this?"

She playfully smacked his hand. "Don't. I said surprise."

He poked his lip out.

"So, how'd the unpacking go?"

"Let's put it this way, I know all there is to know about every item."

Hope grinned. "Sounds like a little girl."

"I had no idea."

Grace raced into the kitchen. "Whatcha got?" She stood on tiptoes.

Hope tweaked the girl's nose. "You're just as nosy as he is." She jabbed her thumb his way.

Sean's chest warmed. Hope did something to him, though for the life of him, he couldn't quite pinpoint what that something was.

She reached into one of the bags and pulled out an oblong box. "How about some spaghetti and French bread?"

Grace clapped. "Yeah. Can I help?"

"Of course. Everybody can help." Hope looked Sean in the eyes. "Where are your pots and pans and a cookie sheet?"

"I've gotcha covered."

Chatter and giggles echoed throughout the condo as they worked together to prepare the meal. What had Sean missed by living alone?

They stuffed themselves with pasta and bread. Sean pushed back from the table. "I'm full. I can't eat another bite. But, my compliments to the chefs." He tipped his head to Grace and then Hope.

"I brought cookies." Hope's eyebrows wiggled.

Sean puffed out his cheeks.

Hope grinned. "Maybe later." She stood, stacking dishes. "I brought a movie I think you might like, Grace."

"What is it?" Grace's eyes bulged.

"It's a princess movie."

"Can I watch it now?"

Hope glanced at Sean, raising her eyebrows.

"Well, sure."

Hope went back to clearing the table.

"Why don't you get Grace set up watching the movie, and we'll get this cleaned up?"

Sean started the DVD and joined Hope in the kitchen. "Hope, I don't know how to thank you."

"You just did." She leaned against the counter and gazed toward the living room. "She's really precious."

He crossed his arms. "I've got to tell my parents about her."

"You sound like you dread that. Sean, they'll adore her."

"I guess it's the initial shame. I mean, I was never married to Tiffany, and I know how they feel about that."

"They won't punish her or you for that. What's done is done, and they need to know they have another grandchild. Not to mention the help grandparents can be."

"Will you come with us? I was thinking about tomorrow when they get home from church."

Her pulse kicked up a notch. "I don't know, Sean. I might be in the way."

"No, you won't. Please." He clasped his hands together like a beggar.

Hope rolled her eyes. "Okay."

Just as Hope and Sean had the kitchen back in order, Grace slid around the corner.

"Hey, are you all ready for cookies now?"

Hope put her finger to her chin as if in deep thought. "Hmm, let me think." She glanced at Sean for his reaction.

"I've never been one who could pass up chocolate chip cookies, especially warm and gooey ones straight from the oven."

"Well, I guess that settles it. Time for cookies."

After eating several cookies, the area around Grace's mouth was splotched with chocolate. Her shirt hadn't avoided goopy chocolate stains either. Hope giggled at Grace's appearance. Had any of the chocolate chips actually made it inside her mouth?

"Looks like someone needs a bath."

"Me?" Grace poked a finger into her chest.

"Yes, you. It's a good thing I brought you some bath supplies, or we might've had to take you outside and use a garden hose."

Grace giggled.

Hope looked at Sean. "Why don't you wrap the rest of our cookies and wait for us in the living room?"

Sean mouthed a thank you and winked. A little shiver trickled down Hope's back.

Hope headed home after the bath and settling plans to meet Sean and Grace after church to visit the Holland's. Her apartment was especially quiet and lonely tonight, so she went to bed early. Her mind wandered back through the events of the day. Did God intend for her to be a mother some day? Would she ever have a family? She could pretend that the three of them were a cozy little family, but they weren't. She swallowed at the lump in her throat. She wasn't sure how she had gotten in the middle of Sean's life again, but she didn't relish the thought of being hurt by him. Surely God would guard her heart while she did whatever He willed her to do in this situation. She had always been open to His calling, but never had such an emotional stir as Sean and now Grace evoked inside her.

CHAPTER ELEVEN

SEAN MISSED HOPE soon after she left for home. Not her help, but her presence. Grace skipped back into the living room. After her bath, Hope had helped her dry her hair and put on her pajamas.

"Can I watch the end of the princess movie now?" Her feathery lashes fluttered.

Sean glanced at his watch. "I think that would be fine. Then, we'll have to get to bed. Hope is going to drop by after church, so we can take you to meet your grandparents."

Grace sat on the couch and pulled her legs under her. Her brow knotted. "Don't you go to church?"

"Well..." Sean hesitated.

"Me and mommy went to church. My Sunday school teacher was real smart about Bible stories."

"Maybe we'll see about you going next time."

"Hope goes, right?"

"Right."

Grace shrugged. "Maybe we could go with her?"

"We'll see." Sean hurriedly hit the play button to start Grace's movie again.

Tiffany had taken Grace to church. Was he expected to carry on with that?

He wasn't sure he was willing to raise his daughter on the Christian principles he had rejected. His chest tightened. If he was going to attempt this father role, he wanted to do it right. His parents had done a good job raising his brother and him. There was more to consider here than just what to feed a five-year-old child and keeping her and her clothes clean.

The movie's credits began to roll, and Sean punched the button to stop it and turn off the television.

"Time for bed." Sean stood.

"You'll stay with me until I fall asleep, right?" She bit her bottom lip.

"Okay. You go ahead, and I'll be there in a minute."

She scooted off the couch and sprinted down the hall. He flicked off lights and checked the door lock. He headed down the hallway but stopped short when he heard Grace talking.

"Dear God, please tell mommy that I'm doing okay. I don't want her to worry. I want her to be happy there in heaven. My Sunday school teacher said that when people go to heaven, we can be happy 'cause we'll see them again. I'm glad 'cause I really miss mommy. Thank You, God, for Mr. Sean and Miss Hope. Amen."

Sean's eyes misted. He massaged his temples. Grace needed to go to church. He couldn't take the hope of seeing her mother again away from her. He composed himself and entered Grace's room.

He perched on the side of the queen-size bed until she fell asleep, which took only moments. He lingered, studied her peaceful expression, and pushed a lock of hair off her cheek. For Grace's sake, he hoped there truly was a heaven.

You know there is, Sean.

He shook his head and quietly eased off the bed.

Sean and Grace were dressed, but Grace insisted he fix her hair in the small ponytail like Mommy always did. She tried to explain the process, but his attempts left much to be desired. He sighed with relief when Hope arrived. He handed her the comb and motioned toward Grace's head. "Can you do this thing?"

Hope covered her mouth with her hand and her shoulders shook slightly when her gaze fell on Sean's latest hairdo attempt. He shrugged. "I have no idea."

"Here now, we can fix this."

Hope talked through the steps as she made a perfect small ponytail holding back the front portion of Grace's blonde locks.

"Do you have a ribbon?"

"Oh, yeah." Grace raced off.

"Thank you. I'm not much of a hair stylist, I'm afraid."

Hope waved her hand dismissively. "You'll learn."

As she tied the ribbon around the ponytail, Sean admired Hope still dressed in the clothes she had worn to church that morning. Her slender skirt and heels made her appear taller. The rust-colored short jacket brought out copper flecks in her green eyes. Her hair lay in soft curls on her shoulders. She and Grace were so natural together.

Grace stood straight and smoothed her dress. "Do I look pretty?"

"Yes, you both do." The compliment slipped out before Sean could stop it. Hope lowered her gaze and her cheeks reddened.

"Good." Grace gave an emphatic nod and reached for Sean's hand. When he grasped it, she extended her hand to Hope. Hope accepted her hand and beamed.

Pulling into his parent's driveway, his pulse sped up. Would they show disappointment in him when he revealed Grace? Only one way to find out. Grace bounded up the sidewalk and onto the front porch. She turned and cocked her head as Hope and Sean made their way up the walk.

When he mounted the porch, he stared at the front door.

"Do you want me to knock?" Grace peered up at him.

"Sure, go ahead."

His mother opened the door and smiled. "Hello, Sean and Hope. And?"

"Grace," the little girl announced emphatically.

"Come in."

When they had settled in the den with his father, Sean drew in a breath and let it out. "Mom and Dad, I wanted to bring Grace by to meet you. Her mother was Tiffany Williams. Now, Grace is with me...because I'm her father."

Mom's hand flew to her chest, and her mouth formed into an O. Dad cocked one eyebrow and glanced at his wife.

Grace slid to the edge of the couch, tilted her head, and trained her eyes on the couple. "See, my mommy went to heaven, so I had to have another place to live."

Sean's mother reached her arms toward Grace, and the little girl stepped into her embrace. As his mom stroked the child's hair, she focused her gaze on Sean and smiled.

Grace pulled back, looking at his mother.

"It is so nice to meet you, Grace. You can call me Nana, and he's Grandpa." She pointed at Sean's father.

No critical words or disgusted expressions. Just acceptance. Grace leaned toward Nana and tried to whisper. "I need to go potty."

Hope stood. "I'll show her." She glanced at Sean and winked. "We'll be right back."

Sean waited until the two had left the room, and then he turned to his parents. "I didn't know about her until a few days ago when

Tiffany's lawyer called. It seems there's really no one else for her except a grandmother who is too disabled to care for her." He ran his hand through his hair. "And, thank goodness for Hope." He chuckled. "I know nothing about taking care of a five-year-old girl."

His father leaned forward. "Son, we'll help you."

His mother grinned. "There is no way you can deny that sweet girl. She looks just like you."

A lump formed in Sean's throat. Their unconditional love was quite unexpected.

This is the love I, too, have for you.

The hair on the back of his neck stood up.

He was glad Grace raced back into the room. She stood toe-to-toe with him and looked him in the eyes.

"Do you know they have a huge-mongous tub in their potty?" Her eyes bugged.

Sean mashed his lips together to stop a laugh. "Yes, I did."

"You just might have to take a dip in that big tub someday soon," Grandpa said.

Nana jumped to her feet and clasped her hands. "Now, who's hungry? I have ham."

Grace raised her hand. "Oooh, I like ham."

Sean's mother grasped the child's hand and led her toward the kitchen. Both chattered as they went.

Sean's father stood, and Sean and Hope followed. His father took a step but turned back, and took Sean into his arms. Sean returned the embrace. His eyes stung, but he blinked back the threatening tears.

Unconditional and everlasting love. It's still there.

His chest ached and longed for the empty spot there to be filled again. But, he pushed the urge aside. The events of the last few days and his lack of sleep wreaked havoc on his emotions.

CHAPTER TWELVE

HOPE PULLED HER car into a parking space in front of Sean's condo. He had asked her if she would take Grace to church. She had agreed but prayed with earnest that he would also attend. As Hope stepped from her driver side, Sean opened the door of his condo.

"Hey, I saw you pull up. Grace is almost ready, but you should probably check her hair."

Hope immediately noticed Sean's casual dress. A heaviness weighed in her chest. Grace rushed in front of her as soon as she stepped inside the door. The little girl spun around. "I think he did a good job on my hair this time. What do you think, Hope?"

"Hmmm. I think you're right. He's learning, huh?"

"Yep." Grace smiled wide.

Sean bowed dramatically, waving his arm in front of him like a devoted knight. As he stood straight again, he looked Hope in the eyes. "Thank you for taking Grace with you." He diverted his gaze. "She needs to go."

"You're welcome."

"When you two get back, I'm taking us out for Sunday lunch."

Hope didn't want him to feel he owed her in any way. "No, I can pick up something."

"Nonsense, I want you to come."

His gaze met hers and melted away at her resolve to not allow him to get to her. She sighed. "Okay. We'll be back a little after noon."

Sean was ready when Hope and Grace returned. The three piled into his car, and Grace chattered about her Sunday school teacher and all of the boys and girls she had met. She barely slowed while eating. As they finished their meal, Grace switched the tone of her monologue.

"You know what? A girl got baptatized today. Can I do that?"

The color drained from Sean's face, and his Adam's apple bobbed as he swallowed. Would he answer her? It wasn't Hope's place to jump in, though she wanted to. The waitress appeared with the ticket, which jolted Sean from his silent daze.

He waved the bill. "I'll pay this and meet you all at the car."

Hope stood, grabbed her purse, took Grace's hand, and led her outside.

The car was quiet as Sean pulled from the restaurant parking lot.

"I just remembered something," Hope said. "Grace's Sunday school teacher asked where she would be attending kindergarten."

Sean glanced at Hope and then quickly back to the road. "Kindergarten? Good grief. I didn't think about her being old enough for school."

"I'm five," Grace said emphatically.

"The church has kindergarten classes. It's really a good program." Hope bit her lip. Sean might not want Grace to go to a church school.

"What do I need to do?" His tone suggested interest.

"I can get you a brochure."

"Yeah, that would be great. Not to change the subject, but I just remembered this. My mom and dad are having a cookout next Sunday afternoon. They wondered if you'd come?"

Did Sean want her to go or was this an invitation only from his parents? Could she continue to be near Sean without giving in to her attraction to him?

"You hafta come," Grace called from the backseat.

Sean grinned. "Yeah, you hafta come."

"I know, we can all go to church together and then to the picnic." Grace's voice was animated. "Please?"

Sean's grin was gone. "We'll see."

Hope silently cheered Grace on.

SUNDAY MORNING SEAN awaited Hope's arrival donned in khakis and a blazer. Grace had finally worn him down over the last several weeks. He would attend church with her and Hope today. What could it hurt? Lots of the people who sat in the pews were just as much a hypocrite as he was. The only difference was he wouldn't pretend to be saintly on Sunday and then live opposite the other six days. He was going to appease Grace.

Hope's gaze scanned him head to toe, and her eyes widened.

"Yes, I'm going with you today, but don't expect it to become a habit."

A smile lit Hope's face, weakening his knees. Did she know what she did to him? But, her faith was central in her life, which meant he had a zero percent chance. His parents had preached against Christians being yoked with unbelievers. How ironic, he still remembered the lingo.

With Grace dropped off at Children's Church, he followed Hope to the sanctuary. As he entered the double doors, his stomach tightened. He took a deep breath and let it out. What was wrong with him? He wouldn't explode or be struck by lightning.

He spotted his mother up ahead. She blinked her eyes, and her mouth gaped.

"Hello, Mother."

She barreled toward him, grabbing him in an embrace. She pulled back. "I'm glad you're here."

"Your granddaughter wore me down this time."

Identifying Grace as her granddaughter had slipped out unexpectedly. It was true, but the reality had yet to sink in for him. He was a daddy.

They took their seats on the Holland pew. After similar shocked reactions to his presence from his brother and sister-in-law, the service began.

Everything went well until the pastor began speaking on the prodigal son.

"That son strayed, but his new lifestyle didn't turn out as well as he thought. It seemed good at first, but it let him down."

The empty place inside Sean screamed out in response to the pastor's words. He shifted in the seat.

"The Bible says that the young man came to the end of himself, came to his senses, and headed back to his father's house."

The pastor moved from behind the pulpit and descended to the floor. Was his gaze fixed on Sean? Sean's hands were wet. He swiped them on his khakis.

"Folks, let me bring it to a personal level."

Sean's chest tightened.

"We stray from our Heavenly Father, because the world lures us and seems promising. But we quickly discover that it doesn't satisfy or fulfill our longing."

Sweat trickled down the back of Sean's neck.

[69]

"The wonderful thing is when we realize this world won't fulfill, our Heavenly Father awaits us with open arms."

Sean's pulse pounded in his ears.

The congregation stood for a time of invitation. Sean gripped the back of the pew in front of him and resisted the draw of the altar. He leaned near Hope's ear and whispered. "Could you get Grace? I'll meet you at the car."

He dashed for the exit and sprinted to the car. He leaned against the driver-side door and took a deep breath to calm his pounding heart.

HOPE RUSHED TO the car after the benediction. His grip on the pew-back and his hustled retreat from the sanctuary proved to her that God was getting through to Sean. Between the Lord and Grace tugging at his heart, surely he would see the Light and return to a relationship with Christ. She struggled not to pray for this turn around for her own selfish motives. This wasn't about her attraction or compatibility. This was about Sean's heart, eternity, and relationship with the Heavenly Father.

Still a desire burned to be more than just a help with Grace's care.

When she arrived at Sean's car, he was already buckled in. She secured Grace in the back and slid into the passenger seat.

Sean made no eye contact. "I thought we might want to change clothes before we head to the picnic at mom and dad's house." His tone was even and deliberate.

"That's a good idea. I brought some jeans and a T-shirt. They're in my car back at your place." She studied his profile.

"Great. Okay." His gaze concentrated forward as he started the car and headed out of the parking lot.

All was silent until Grace's little high-pitched voice began telling about everything that had happened during Children's Church. As she chattered on, Sean's shoulders and face visibly softened.

Would Hope have the opportunity to talk to him about the sermon's effect on him? Should she? She raised a silent prayer for guidance.

HOPE ABSORBED THE family atmosphere at the Hollands'. She listened to the banter of the adults and the giggles from Grace and Miranda's play. Tears stung her eyes, but she blinked them back, scolding her envy. The sun drooped low as evening approached.

"We better get going. Grace starts kindergarten tomorrow," Sean announced.

A drawn-out whine emitted from the two girls.

"Aw, come on, the two of you will be in the same class in the morning," Sean's brother, Richard, cut in.

At that reminder the two girls clasped hands, jumped up and down, and squealed. Sean stuck a finger in his ear and pursed his lips. "Not used to that yet."

Hope chuckled.

As they made their way to the car, Sean lightly touched Hope's elbow. "You'll stay long enough to help with Grace's bath, won't you?"

"Sure." Hope nodded.

They had just started the short drive to Sean's when Grace spoke up from the back seat. "Did you know that Miranda got saved and babtatized?"

"Um, yeah, I think I remember Nana telling me about that," Sean said.

"Well, I want to be saved and babtatized, too. I love Jesus."

Sean's hands tightened on the steering wheel, his knuckles whitened. Hope's pulse kicked up a notch. She silently asked God if she should speak, but his Spirit held her back.

Sean paused. Would Hope answer Grace's question and get him off the hook? Somewhere deep inside, his resistance let go like the tumbling of a brick wall. A warmth spread through his chest like a wave suddenly set free. In his spirit he uttered, *Oh God.*

That was the only invitation needed. He pulled into a parking space at his condo complex, switched off the engine, and turned to face Grace.

"Sweetie, do you know that Jesus died for you?"

"Yeah. I know that. He died for me, and I ask Him to forgive my bad stuff, and then He comes to live in me and help me. And, one day I'll go to Heaven to see Mommy."

Hope sniffed. Sean glanced at her. Tears flowed down her cheeks. Her eyes met his. He returned his gaze to Grace. "I do believe you've got it. Have you prayed and told Him this? Have you asked Him into your heart?"

"No, but I can right here, right?"

Sean shrugged. "Sure."

Grace extended her hands, one toward him, the other toward Hope. "Give me your hands."

They each took one of her hands. Sean reached for Hope's other hand, meeting her gaze. She grasped his hand and smiled though tears that trickled down her face. He looked back at Grace, nodded, and bowed his head. His daughter's prayer rang with pure child-like faith. A knot formed in his throat. Sean hadn't been privy to Grace's birth, but God had provided him this special moment of her new birth.

He couldn't suppress the Truth any longer.

When Grace said amen, Sean burst from his seat, grabbing her from her booster. He held her close and swung her around in circles.

Hope appeared at his side. He wrapped her waist with one arm, still holding Grace in the other, and squeezed. No words came as he looked into Hope's glistening eyes. They finally made their way inside. Hope looked from Grace to him. "I'm so proud and happy for both of you." Her lip quivered.

He gazed into Hope's eyes. "Honestly, I think it took more faith not to believe."

After her bath, Grace couldn't keep her eyes open. Sean picked her up and carried her limp body to her bed. Hope followed, stepping in front of him to turn down the bed covers. As he eased her onto her pillow, her lips curled into a slight smile. Sean stifled a laugh.

"I love you, Daddy." Her voice was low but clear. Sean's breath caught in his throat. She snuggled her stuffed bear, and her breathing became immediately even.

He glanced at Hope and motioned toward the hall with a nod. Standing outside Grace's door, he gazed in. "That's the first time she's called me Daddy," he whispered.

CHAPTER THIRTEEN

SEAN'S CELL PHONE buzzed as he got back into his car after dropping Grace at school. He glanced at the screen. Mrs. Collins, the lawyer. *Wonder why she's calling?*

"Hello, this is Sean Holland."

"Mr. Holland, this is Mrs. Collins." Her voice was serious. "Do you have a moment today to stop by my office?"

"Yes. Are you available right now?"

"Yes, that would be fine."

"Do I need to know something?"

"I'd prefer to speak to you in person, if you don't mind."

Sean's stomach tightened. What was this all about? He clenched the steering wheel and pushed beyond the speed limit. Stepping into the law office's lobby, he was escorted directly to Mrs. Collin's office. She stood, extending her hand. After a quick shake, she plopped back into her desk chair.

"Please, have a seat."

Sean eased into one of two chairs facing the desk. "What's this all about?"

"I wanted to make sure you knew that Grace's grandmother is planning on filing for custody."

"But I was appointed her guardian in the will."

"Yes, however, she can file. Between you and me, Mrs. Williams has recently remarried, and she discovered there is money set aside for Grace. I think that's what she's after."

"But, she doesn't have a chance, right?" Sean scooted to the edge of the seat.

"Well, she is a relative. Your name isn't on Grace's birth certificate."

"Mrs. Collins, cut to the chase. We both know Tiffany wanted Grace with me."

"Of course, it would look better if you were married, but…" She shook her head. "You'll appear in front of a judge who will decide what's best."

"So, we're fine?"

"A lot depends on which judge presides and how well Mrs. Williams presents herself and her husband as a better home."

Sean's throat constricted.

"I'll be in touch," the lawyer said.

Sean trudged to his car and sat in the driver's seat, his forehead on the steering wheel. He couldn't lose Grace now. She called him Daddy. He was starting to get the hang of a little girl's routine and even fixing hair. How could he make sure he kept his little girl? His mind whirled. He sighed and raised his head. There was one way.

HOPE RUSHED TO shower and change. Sean had called and asked her to supper. His tone was guarded or serious. She couldn't quite determine which, but there was something about his voice that let her know this would be more than just dining out. He had even arranged for Grace to stay with his parents. There was a knock on her door. She glanced at her watch. He was early. Her stomach quivered, and she gnawed her bottom lip. She took a deep breath, plastered on a smile, and flung the door open.

"Hi. I'm a bit early. Sorry about that." Sean ducked his head slightly and gazed at her, brows raised.

Hope shook her head. "It's fine. I'll just be a minute. Have a seat." She jogged back to the bathroom and brushed through her hair again. She stared at her reflection, then rolled her eyes. Did Sean have any feelings toward her other than as a friend and help with Grace? She had to know. Soon.

Maybe tonight would afford a moment to discover his intentions. Could she be brave enough to ask? Would his answer hurt? She prayed for direction and courage.

After being seated at a local restaurant, Sean leaned forward, locking her gaze with his.

"Something's come up with Grace." He paused, a pained expression on his face.

Hope instinctively placed her hand on his arm. "What is it?"

"Tiffany's mother has remarried and obviously found out there is money set aside for Grace. She's going to try to get custody."

Hope's chest tightened. "But, you have the letter, so she can't follow through, right?"

"My lawyer says it depends on the judge and which is deemed more of a family." He ran his fingers through his hair and plopped his arm back onto the table. "I have to look like the better home." His gaze bore into her. He kept silent as if awaiting a reply.

"Did the lawyer give you any advice on what to do?"

Sean nodded, and his eyes darted everywhere except to her.

Hope leaned over the table closer to him, forcing his gaze to meet hers. "Sean, tell me."

"She said I would fare better if I were married, giving Grace two parents."

Hope's heart flip-flopped. Was he saying what she thought he was saying?

He reached for her hand, grasping it and caressing it with his thumb. "I can't believe I would even ask this of you, but it's all I can think about."

A tremble spread through her body.

"And, I actually feel it would be good for Grace. Besides, we spend a lot of time together anyway." He paused and sat up straighter. "Would you marry me? For Grace's sake?"

Just for Grace's sake? Would this be a complete disaster? Sean hadn't mentioned love for her. Should she question that? She feared his answer. But, Hope couldn't imagine the horror for Grace if she were to lose another parent. Could her heart handle a fake marriage when she really yearned for the real thing with Sean? Where was that warning feeling from the Holy Spirit she was sure she should feel? "Okay…yes."

Sean's face lit up, and his eyes danced. He grabbed both of her hands and squeezed. "I thought we could talk to the preacher, maybe do it in his office."

Hope nodded.

CHAPTER FOURTEEN

A WEEK LATER, Hope stood next to Sean in the pastor's office flanked by Sean's parents and Grace as witnesses. The ceremony was short and sweet. When the pastor announced that Sean could kiss his bride, Hope's breath caught in her throat.

Sean gazed into her eyes. His expression softened, and he planted a soft kiss on her lips, causing a tingling sensation to spread through her chest. He embraced her, and the warmth and feel of his body pressed to hers was nearly intoxicating. Tears stung her eyes. How could he be such a good actor? That felt like the real thing. She wished it were.

The tender moment ended with hugs and congratulations. Little arms wrapped Hope's leg. She knelt and Grace engulfed her in a hug.

"I do wish you would at least let us take Grace tonight so you two can be alone," Sean's mother said.

Sean glanced at Hope and then looked at Mrs. Holland. "We'll get the opportunity later. Work schedules aren't conducive right now."

Grace's hand slipped into Hope's and reached for Sean's. "Let's go eat. Today we should get dessert because it's a special 'ccasion."

Sean smiled and winked at Hope. "Sounds good to me."

Eating at the restaurant felt normal. The three of them had done that often. Going back to Sean's condo would be quite different. He had solved the sleeping arrangements. Hope would take his bed while Sean would sleep in the room that also held his office. She couldn't help lamenting over the way she had dreamed a real wedding night would be. That night she lay in Sean's bed twisting the unfamiliar band on her finger. Sean slept just across the hall. She craved the warmth of his embrace.

That first week they had fallen into a routine which eased the awkward newness of this new arrangement. Hope's only problem? How long until Sean saw through her ruse and realized she was truly in love with him?

SEAN ENJOYED HAVING Hope near these six weeks, but wished for more. Would she back off if she knew he wanted this to be a real marriage?

With Grace dropped off at kindergarten, his work screamed for attention. He planned to lock himself in his home office until time to pick his daughter up again. He slid into his parking space, and his head whipped to Hope's car. Why was she still here? Was she ill? He raced to the door and let himself in just as Hope emerged from the bathroom wrapped in a towel. Her eyes bulged.

She certainly didn't appear ill. Sean's pulse raced. He swallowed. "I'm sorry. Um, are you okay?" He ran his hand down his face. He resisted going to her, touching her. "I just saw your car and thought…"

Her cheeks reddened, and she pulled the towel tighter around her body. "Oh, I'm so sorry. I don't have a shift today." Her eyes darted. "I can get out of your way."

"No." That came out too soon. Her freshly scrubbed face glowed. "I mean, no, you're not in the way. This is your home too."

Hope mashed her lips together and stared at the ceiling as if contemplating his words. Her gaze focused on him. "Thank you." Her voice was low and shaky.

He was messing this up. What more could he say to make her believe what he had said?

"Excuse me." She turned and rushed down the hall.

Sean plopped onto the couch and took a deep breath to calm his pounding heart. Why couldn't he just admit to her that he wanted to make a home with her? *Wake up, Holland, you're not good enough for her.* He jumped to his feet and retreated to his writing hole, unsure he could focus now.

HOPE PLANTED HER back to the bedroom door. Her hands trembled, and her breath came in pants. Her heart had prompted her to run into Sean's arms. But, her fear of rejection held her fast. This game of pretend chipped away at her piece by piece. How long could she live with a man she had fallen in love with but didn't return her affections? Could he learn to love her?

"I'M GOING TO pick up Grace," he called through Hope's bedroom door. She hadn't emerged all afternoon.

"Okay." Her muffled voice came through the wall.

Sean trudged to his car. Could they continue like this?

His phone buzzed through his car's system. He glanced at the screen. The lawyer.

"Mrs. Collins, hello."

"Mr. Holland, I'm glad I could catch you before the weekend. Tiffany's mother has dropped everything, so Grace remains in your care."

"That's great." His voice lacked the enthusiasm.

"Is everything, okay?"

"Oh, yeah. Sorry. I'm surprised she gave up so soon."

"Yes, it's true. Have a nice day and congratulations."

"I will, and thanks." He ended the call. Would Hope leave now? Get an annulment? His heart ached.

He waited until Grace was asleep that evening and then led Hope into the living room, sitting next to her on the couch.

Her brow crinkled.

"I got a call from the lawyer today."

"Oh?"

"It seems that Tiffany's mother has backed down."

Hope bowed her head. Did her lip quiver? She stood quickly and smiled. "That's good then." She shrugged.

Sean rubbed his chin and sighed. "I guess I didn't need to panic like I did."

"I understand. You didn't force me." She rushed from the room and into her bedroom. Was she that eager to leave? She emerged with one suitcase. "I'll get the other stuff tomorrow. I'm sure you're ready to be back in your own room."

Her eyes were red-rimmed. A tear rolled down her cheek, and she hurriedly swiped it with the back of her hand. Why the tears? Would she miss Grace? Could she possibly miss him? She opened the door, walked out, and never looked back.

His heart ached. He had to stop her, had to try. His pulse pounded as he sped for the parking lot.

"Wait!" He was too late.

TEARS BLURRED HOPE'S vision as she sped from Sean's condo. Why did her heart have to ache like that? She had fooled herself thinking Sean might actually love her enough to stay married. Why had she so desperately jumped at his proposal, knowing it could end so soon? She knew the answer. She craved a family, a life that she'd never had. *God, why didn't your Spirit stop me?*

She slowed to a stop at a red light and swiped tears from her eyes with the backs of her hands. The light turned green, and she accelerated into the intersection. A loud horn blared, and she glanced to her left. The front grill of a large truck barreled toward her. Her breath caught in her throat. Knowing it was too close to get out of the way, Hope stiffened her body and closed her eyes, anticipating the impact.

"Dear God!" she screamed.

CHAPTER FIFTEEN

SEAN JOLTED WHEN his cell phone rang. He picked it up quickly. He didn't want Grace to awaken. He wasn't prepared to explain where Hope had gone.

"Hello." He cleared his throat and repeated his greeting. He glanced at his watch. Midnight.

"Is this Mr. Sean Holland?" The voice sounded serious and direct.

"Yes, it is."

"Mr. Holland, your wife has been in a serious accident. We need you to come to the Emergency Room at Baptist Hospital immediately."

Sean's stomach hardened, his heart raced and nearly exploded.

"Sir?"

"I'm sorry. Yes, I'll be there." Sean ended the call and slipped into his shoes. Just as he reached for the doorknob, he remembered Grace. What should he do? He couldn't leave her alone, and he definitely couldn't take her with him. He fumbled with his phone, finally locating his parent's number. Hurry. Hurry.

"Son?" His father's voice answered.

"Dad, I need you and mom to come stay with Grace. Hope's been in an accident. I have to get to the ER."

"What happened?"

"I don't have time to explain. I just know that it's serious, and I need to get there."

"We're on our way."

Sean paced a path back and forth from the living room to the front door. His whole body trembled. What took his parents so long?

He should've caught Hope. He should've never let her go. *Please don't die.* His eyes misted. He jumped at tapping on the door. He swung it open to his parent's distressed, wide-eyed faces.

"Thank you. Grace is asleep in her bed. I'll call when I know something."

"We love you, Son," his mother called to him as he sprinted for his car.

The drive to the hospital had never been so long. Finally, he screeched his car into a parking space, ran into the ER entrance, and straight to one of three cubicles.

"My wife, Hope. They called me."

"Mr. Holland?"

He nodded, struggling to catch his breath.

"I'll meet you at the double doors." The woman gestured to his left.

He stepped to where she indicated, heard a buzz, and the doors opened. The woman motioned him through and directed his attention to some forms.

"We need you to sign these…"

Sean grabbed the pen and scribbled his signature without looking. "Can I see her?"

"Wait here just a moment."

Sean couldn't stand still. He shifted his feet and stuck his trembling hands into his pockets.

The nurse reappeared and looked him directly in the eyes. "Mr. Holland, it might be disturbing to see your wife. I want to warn you."

Sean swallowed at the lump in his throat.

"She's pretty banged up."

"What happened? Do you know?"

"A truck ran through an intersection, striking your wife's car on the driver's side."

Sean's stomach lurched. "Oh, God, no," he whispered.

"You can see her for just a moment, then you'll need to wait outside. The medical staff tending her need their space. They're doing everything they can."

Sean nodded and followed the nurse into a cubicle. Doctors and nurses buzzed around a gurney. He spotted Hope's swollen and bloodied face. Covering his gaping mouth to hide his shock, he slid next to her. Hot tears streamed down his cheeks. He whispered her name and pushed a lock of hair from her forehead.

"Sir, I'm going to have to ask you to wait out in the waiting room."

"But…"

"We'll keep you informed."

Two hands on his arms guided him from the room. He meandered to a vacant corner of the waiting room and plopped onto a black vinyl chair. He squeezed his eyes shut and silently prayed. "I know I have no right asking You for anything, but please spare her. I love her."

The ticking of the clock on the wall above his head accentuated each grueling moment with no word from the doctors. Finally, about 6:30 a.m., a doctor strode Sean's direction. The doctor's face appeared quite grave. Sean stood.

"Mr. Holland?"

Sean nodded. "How is she?"

"She's alive."

Sean let out a breath.

"But, she's being transferred to the ICU upstairs. We're concerned about brain swelling and possible internal injuries. Because of the trauma, we're keeping her sedated."

"Can I see her? Be with her?"

"Of course. I want to limit a lot of other visitors. But, you being her husband, we're a little more lenient with the closest family member in these kinds of situations."

Sean's stomach wrenched tighter.

"A nurse will come for you in a little while."

Sean's phone vibrated in his pocket. He pulled it out. "Dad?"

"Son, how is Hope?"

"They're moving her to ICU. A truck struck her in the driver's side. She's alive, but it's serious." Grace's little-girl voice chirped in the background. "About Grace . . ."

"Your mom and I will take her home with us."

"I would appreciate it. I feel I need to stay here." Sean ran his hand through his hair.

"She wants to talk to you."

"Put her on."

"Hello?"

"Grace, honey, Hope's been in a car wreck, so I'm going to stay with her here at the hospital."

"Can I come stay, too?"

"I'm afraid they won't let little girls be here, but you go with Nana and Grandpa. I'll see you soon."

"But, will God take her away and not let me see her? That's what happened with Mommy." Her voice quivered. "She needs the shawl."

The prayer shawl.

"Let me talk with Grandpa again, okay?"

"Son."

"Dad, on the way to your house, could you stop by? Grace wants to bring the prayer shawl."

"Sure, Son."

Sean would meet them outside the hospital entrance, letting the ER receptionist know. He didn't want to miss the nurse who would take him to Hope's room. He spotted the familiar SUV and stepped out the door onto the sidewalk. Before he walked two steps, Grace's little feet patted over, and she threw her arms around his legs. He knelt, and she wrapped her arms about his neck. Sean returned the embrace and breathed in the clean smell of her hair.

She stepped back and pushed the prayer shawl towards him. "Hope needs this, Daddy."

Sean's heart fluttered at her use of Daddy again. "I'll take it to her."

The little girl's bottom lip trembled. Crocodile tears rushed down her cheeks. "Car wrecks take mommies away."

Sean choked back tears, clearing his throat. He ran his hand through her hair and settled it on her shoulder and squeezed it. "Honey, we'll pray that won't happen."

"Right now?" Her little eyes pleaded.

He glanced at his father, who nodded, urging him. Fixing his gaze on Grace, he breathed in and let it out. Grace grabbed both his hands and closed her eyes and bowed her head. Sean swallowed at the lump in his throat. He joined her by closing his eyes and bowing. "Dear God, please heal Hope. We love her and want her to be okay."

Looking into Grace's face, she nodded and embraced him around the neck again. When she pushed back, he swiped her cheeks. "You don't mind staying with Nana and Grandpa do you?"

Grace shook her head. "No. Hope needs you."

Sean's chest tightened. He touched her cheek. "I'll call you later. Okay?"

"Okay." She leaned in and whispered. "I'll be good."

"I'm counting on that." He tweaked her nose then glanced at his parents. "I'm more worried about Nana and Grandpa." He winked.

After hugs and promises to call to keep them updated, Sean waved as the three drove away.

CHAPTER SIXTEEN

SEAN CLUTCHED THE shawl and marched back to his spot in the waiting room. After what seemed to be hours, the nurse finally escorted him to the ICU room where Hope was now settled. Her body appeared frail in the large bed. Tubes and chords attached her to numerous machines replete with small blinking lights and humming noises.

He stared at her battered face, squeezed the prayer shawl, and whispered a prayer. "God, I love her. Please spare her. I need her." Tears slid down his cheeks and dripped onto his shirt. "She was right. I can't get through something like this without you."

He spread the shawl over Hope's chest and sat in the only chair in the small room, never taking his gaze from her face.

SEAN'S VIGIL BY Hope's side had been going on for four days now. He had only left a couple of times to shower and change clothes.

"Mr. Holland?" a male voice called from behind.

Sean twisted around in his chair to find the doctor. "Yes?"

"I wanted to let you know that we are going to ease Mrs. Holland off some of the medications we've used to keep her knocked out."

"So, she might wake up?" Sean's pulse picked up a notch.

"We are hoping she will awaken gradually. But, I must warn you that we have no idea of the extent of damage she could have."

"Meaning?"

"Meaning, I'm not sure about possible memory loss or other impairments like speech."

Sean's chest ached, and his whole body trembled. He could only nod. The doctor exited, and Sean turned his attention back to Hope. This precious woman didn't deserve this. He had made such a mess of everything. What if her memory was gone? What if she couldn't speak or had some other permanent impairment? She would blame him and rightfully so. Why couldn't he be laying there in that hospital bed instead of her?

Time to swallow his miserable pride. He yanked his cell phone out of his pocket, bringing up his parent's number.

"Sean, what's happened?" His mother's panicked voice came through.

"Mom, they're going to wean her off the drugs. The doctor's not sure..." His voice broke. "Mama, you've gotta get people praying."

His mother sighed. "Thank God."

"Excuse me?"

"The prodigal returns?"

"Let's just say that Hope helped me realize that it took more faith not to believe in God."

His mother sniffed. "All things work together for good for those who live according to His purpose."

"Oh, Mom, Hope's just got to be all right."

"We're joining in your prayers, Son."

HOPE BECAME RESTLESS as the hours stretched out, rocking her head from side to side or shifting her arms and legs. Still, she hadn't opened her eyes. Each time Sean would caress her arm or speak her name.

Finally, Sean knelt beside her bed. What was that verse his mother had quoted? "All things work together for good—"

"—for those who live according to His purpose. Romans 8:28," Hope said in a low voice.

Sean's head jerked up, and he sprang to his feet just in time to see Hope's eyes flutter. She gazed into his eyes. Sean bit his lip, at a loss for words. Did she recognize him?

"Sean." It came out almost like a sigh.

He couldn't stop a smile. "Hope." Tears blurred his vision. He blinked them aside.

She glanced at the prayer shawl still draped across her chest and then focused back on Sean. "You prayed?"

"I haven't stopped since they called me to the hospital."

Her mouth curved upwards. "Thank God."

Sean chuckled. "You sound like my mother." He gently touched her cheek with his hand. Hope leaned into it. "Do you know why you're here?"

"A big truck."

He chuckled again. "I'm so glad you're awake and know who I am."

Her eyelids fluttered. "I'm sorry. No energy."

He stroked her arm. "That's okay. You rest. I'll be here when you wake up again."

She closed her eyes and nodded. Her breathing became even.

Now it was his turn. "Thank God."

CHAPTER SEVENTEEN

THE DOCTOR INFORMED Hope that she would finally be able to go home after two weeks in the hospital. Sean was determined for her to go back to his condo for the remainder of her recovery. Would it be awkward? Her stomach knotted. She gripped the prayer shawl and prayed for God to calm her spirit and her nerves.

"Hey, Sunshine, you ready to blow this joint?" Sean called as he burst into her room.

"Yep, I believe so."

"Grace is absolutely beside herself with excitement." He shook his head and chuckled. "She had me up this morning before six, ordering me to come get you."

Hope's chest warmed. She studied Sean's face. Did he share Grace's enthusiasm? Or, was this a temporary arrangement until she fully recovered? She bit her bottom lip to stop a sudden rush of moisture in her eyes. Why couldn't it be different? Why couldn't it be as it appeared to everyone else? A family of three.

The ride to the condo was quiet. Sean pulled into the parking space, jumped out, and met her as she struggled to stand up. "Here, let me help you."

"The doctor said I should be able to get rid of the crutches soon."

"Yeah, but right now you need them." He narrowed his gaze at her as if scolding her.

He steadied her with a hand on her waist. Warmth spread through her. Stop. She met his gaze again. "Look, I'm sorry to be so much trouble. I should be out of your hair in a few weeks."

He gazed into her eyes with a pained expression on his face. "Let's get something clear. As far as I'm concerned, I want you to stay in my hair." He chuckled.

"What?"

He stepped closer and took her hand in his. "I hate the thought of you leaving, because…I love you."

Hope's eyes widened, and her free hand covered her mouth.

Sean rubbed the back of his neck. "I know. It's crazy."

She shook her head. "It's not crazy." Tears trickled down her cheeks. "Somewhere in the midst of all of this, I fell in love with you, but…"

Sean put a finger to her lips and stopped her. "No but." He wrapped his arms around her and pressed his lips to hers. She allowed her body to relax into his, then slid her head to his chest. He stroked her back.

Hope's pulse pounded, her heart nearly burst. Sean had actually declared his love for her.

SEAN'S EYES MISTED over. Relief spread through his body like a tonic. Hope loved him.

She pushed back, looking him in the eyes. "What do we do now?"

"Well, Mrs. Holland, this is where I carry you over the threshold right proper like." He scooped her into his arms. She squealed and placed her arms around his neck, burying her face in his shoulder.

This is right, Son.

The hairs on his neck perked.

SIX WEEKS LATER, Hope, minus the crutches, met her groom and Grace in the front of the church filled with family and friends. God was too good. Hope had a family and a home.

They each recited vows they had made in the pastor's office, yet this time both knew the other's heart. Just when Hope thought the ceremony was over, the pastor asked Sean to share a few words.

Her groom held both of her hands and gazed into her eyes. "I had strayed from God, but He pursued me, giving me Hope and Grace." He chuckled. "Puns intended." He reached down, picking up Grace in his left arm. He grasped Hope's hand again with his right, planting a kiss on her lips. "Now, let's eat dessert, because it's a special 'casion."

Grace pumped her fist in the air. "Yessss!"

INHERITANCE

Paula Mowery

CHAPTER ONE

Music chimed from the organ. I opened my bulletin to get the page number for the final hymn. My gaze once again rested upon the sermon title for today, "Trusting God in Everything." Trust God? I didn't have anything left to entrust to Him. Mom was gone. My husband had divorced me for another woman, and yesterday, I'd lost my job. I wasn't sure I could trust God.

At thirty years old, with no special training or schooling of any kind and now no income, I would be out on the streets.

After the benediction, I hurried to my car, plopped into the driver's seat, and mulled over my life or lack of one.

Maybe I should go see Granny. She called almost every day to check up on me. She continued to hint at my visiting. But, I couldn't afford the gas for the car to make the drive from Knoxville to Greeneville and back. Granny would help me, but I needed to make some kind of life on my own, didn't I? I couldn't sneak off to Granny Olivia's world no matter how much I might enjoy the escape. The reality was, I was a single, un-college-educated woman with few prospects.

I shook my head in disgust as I steered into a parking spot at the apartment complex. Granny Olivia would scold me good if she heard me put myself down. And, if I was going to trust him, God needed to help me, because my "everything" was a total mess, and I was pretty angry about it.

I trudged to my apartment door, shoved it open, and slammed it behind me. I kicked off my dress shoes and glanced at the phone screen, shocked to have received a voicemail. I snagged the phone and dialed in my code.

"This message is for Alexandra Lyndon. I regret to inform you that your grandmother, Olivia Lyndon, has had a stroke. You need to come quickly. It's only a matter of time." The formal voice related the hospital's location.

I closed my eyes, stopping hot tears. I let out a breath and opened my eyes. What had I done to deserve all this? Was God going to take the last precious person from me?

ARRIVING AT THE hospital an hour later, I skidded into the first available parking spot. I raced to the information desk inside the hospital entrance where a white-haired lady sat wearing a bright pink shirt.

"I need to find Olivia Lyndon, please."

The woman tilted her head and smiled. "Yes, dear Miss Olivia. She's in ICU—just up..."

I didn't wait for instructions. I sprinted for the elevators and hoped I wasn't too late. Following the signs, I found the double doors leading to the ICU and pressed the call button to the right on the wall.

A voice squawked, "May I help you?"

"Yes. I need to see my granny—Olivia Lyndon."

A nurse emerged, took my arm, and led me to a small room. I slowed when Granny Olivia's fragile form came into view. Her eyes were closed, and her face was pale. Was I too late?

Her eyes fluttered open, and her head turned toward me. A weak smile upturned her mouth. I hurried to her side. "I'm sorry, Granny."

She shook her head and reached for my hand. "My precious, Alex. I love you." Her voice was barely audible. I leaned closer. "I have wanted to tell you..." She closed her eyes and breathed in. She expelled the air and opened her eyes again.

I patted her hand gently. "It's okay. Don't tire yourself. I'm here. Let's get you better."

A crooked smile returned. "No," she whispered. "The card. Call her." Her hand went limp in mine.

Tears gushed like a torrent. "Oh, Granny, don't go." I fixed my gaze on the nurse, standing on the other side of the bed. I couldn't bring myself to ask if this was it.

"She's been slipping in and out of consciousness." She placed something into my hand, squeezing it into my palm. "Here's the card."

I glanced down. It was a lawyer's name and number. I crumpled it in my palm and gazed at Granny one more time. I should have been here long ago. The silence in the room deafened me and only made me more aware that once she was gone I would be utterly alone.

But, I wouldn't accept it. Granny was strong. She just needed time to recover. I shoved the business card into my jeans pocket. I was pretty sure I understood what the lawyer contact was for, but I wouldn't need it.

"Ma'am?" The nurse spoke in a soft tone. "The visiting time is up for now here in the ICU. You'll have to go to the waiting room until the next visitation."

I froze. Now I was being forced to leave her?

The nurse patted my arm. "Should there be any change, I'll come for you." She smiled.

After kissing Granny's forehead, I meandered to a corner chair in the waiting area and slumped into it. My only entertainment choices were a raunchy talk show blaring on the TV or a stack of outdated magazines on the table beside me.

A hospital volunteer carried a basket filled with crackers and snacks. When she offered me a choice, I gladly accepted much to the delight of my grumbling stomach.

During the next visitation time, there was no change in Granny. She just lay there in a deep sleep. I was tempted to shake her. When I did touch her, the nurse informed me that Granny had gone into a coma.

Her life seemed to ebb away just like my courage. If she left, I couldn't get through anything difficult. Not by myself.

At about ten thirty that evening, the few other ICU lounge inhabitants who remained grabbed blankets and pillows they retrieved from a small closet. One of the women extended a blanket and pillow toward me. "Are you staying tonight?"

I nodded and cleared my throat. "Yes. Thank you."

I did my best to stretch out and find some comfortable position in an awkward fold-out chair. Exhaustion finally won out over discomfort.

Bustling in the lounge woke me early the next morning. Time for the first visitation. I slung my legs around and jumped up, smoothing at my hair and crumpled clothing. The line of anxious visitors formed, and I fell in behind. I shuffled to Granny's cubicle and stared at her still motionless body. The nurse's voice echoed from across the room. "Still no change."

I nodded and eased into a nearby chair.

"I'll be right back." She padded out.

Propping my forearms on the bed, I leaned my chin on them. My gaze never left Granny's face. "Please wake up and talk to me," I whispered.

Sounds of families consoling one another reverberated around the walkway outside the cubicle. I shivered. I sat up and clutched my arms across my waist and rocked. *God, if You will just let her wake up and be okay, I'll do whatever You want. Even trust. If that's what it takes, I will.*

"Miss, are you all right?"

My head jerked around.

The nurse had returned. "You need to get something to eat, honey, before the next visitation. You have to take care of yourself."

"Yes, thank you." I shuffled back to the ICU Lounge and plopped into the cold vinyl chair. *Not sure how I'll pay for something to eat.*

"Miss Olivia, Olivia Lyndon. Is this where she is?"

My ears perked at the mention of Granny's name. I stood and hurried over to the desk. "Excuse me, are you looking for Olivia Lyndon?"

The older man spun around and looked me in the eyes. "Why, yes." He leaned closer to my face and narrowed his eyes. "Aren't you her granddaughter?"

"Yes, sir. I'm Alex."

"Boy howdy, yes." He patted my back heartily, knocking the air from my lungs. "I'm Bart Smith. I'm a deacon over at the church."

"So nice of you to come to check on Granny Olivia. Here, let's sit over here." I gestured toward my staked out chair.

Mr. Smith crossed the room in two large strides and plunked into a seat which he dwarfed. He was broad and tall and sported a worn blue blazer whose buttons hadn't attached with the holes in some time. His face was round, covered with a white beard. The hair on his head wound around his head, leaving a smooth shiny top. Rather resembled a jolly Santa Claus. "So, how is Sister Olivia?"

"I'm afraid she's gone into a coma."

Mr. Smith tsked through his teeth. "I'm so sorry." He reached into his coat and produced a white envelope which he extended in my direction. "This is for you. Hospital food is mighty costly."

I held the packet to my chest. "You…I don't know… Thank you. This is so kind."

Mr. Smith jumped to his feet. "I better be getting along. I'll pass this information along to our prayer chain. They'll be prayin'. And, should you need anything, just call me." He shoved a business card into my hand. "That's my deacon card with my number on it."

"Thank you again." I glanced at my watch. Just enough time to run down to the cafeteria for a bite to eat and be back in time for the next visitation.

The visits were always the same. I stared at Granny's unmoving body, willing her to wake up. Nothing changed.

That evening I bedded down again on the awful reclining chair. I squirmed for two hours until falling into a light doze.

I jolted awake at a gentle tap on my shoulder. Squinting, I recognized the nurse and sat straight up.

"Please come with me." Her voice was low and serious.

Springing to my feet, I clumsily followed her into a small room, not the ICU as I expected. A doctor already stood in the room. My heart pounded, rattling my chest.

"Miss Lyndon, I'm sorry. Your grandmother has passed."

My breath caught. This couldn't be happening.

"Do you know about arrangements? Did she have that planned?" The doctor gazed at me and adjusted his glasses.

The card. "I need to make a phone call."

"Okay." The doctor nodded. He and the nurse exited the room, closing the door behind them.

I leaned against the wall and slid my back down until I hit the floor, pulling my knees to my chest. She was really gone. What did I do now? I glanced at my watch—7:15. I squinted at the day and date in the small box on my watch's face. Tuesday. Thank goodness it had that reading. I had no idea what day it was. I pulled myself together long enough to make it to the ICU restroom. I slipped inside and bolted the door. I stared at my reflection in the mirror over the sink. "So much for trust." Tears spilled over my cheeks and dripped off my chin. Sobs shook me to the point that I could hardly catch my breath. I smacked the counter until my hand tingled. Finally, I gritted my teeth and squared my shoulders. I splashed some cold water on my face and tamed my hair with a band I found in my pocket.

I dashed to my car and slid into the driver's seat, pulling out the card the nurse had pressed into my hand. I dialed the phone number on the card and was given directions to a law office.

I steered my car into a parking space in front of the law office and shuffled toward the entrance. I took a deep breath and let it out as I opened the glass door. A tall blonde dressed in a dark pantsuit met me. "Ms. Lyndon?" I nodded. "Follow me."

We stepped into a medium-sized office near the front lobby area. A woman sat at a large desk studying a laptop screen. She glanced in my direction and stood. "Ms. Lyndon, I'm Mrs. Sutton." She offered me a chair with a sweep of her hand. I sat and waited as she looked at a stack of papers on the desk. She peered at me through the top of her glasses. "Mrs. Lyndon had everything planned for the funeral. Will Friday be acceptable? That gives a couple of days to get things set. Does that work for you?"

"Yes, Ma'am." My answer squeaked out. "Do I need to contact...?"

"Hmm? Oh, no. All the arrangements have been taken care of. I knew what to do as soon as I received your call. Your grandmother had it all set up. She didn't want you to have to deal with all of this." Her tone was nonchalant.

I nodded when she gazed at me expectantly.

"Good. It will be at Grace Baptist. Do you know it?" Her voice seemed devoid of emotion—flat.

I nodded. "Yes, that was her church."

"There will be a service at six o'clock. The pastor there obviously has the instructions. Then, I want to read the will here at my office next Thursday. Though there's not much left to say. You have the house." She shrugged. "And, Mrs. Lyndon alluded to the fact that your inheritance was in the Word. At any rate, can you be here? That is the soonest I can get to this."

"Yes." I found myself not hesitating to answer my availability. My apartment in Knoxville was an hour and a half away—not too far to be available when needed. Mrs. Sutton gave me a few other particulars and I left.

My mind whirred with everything Mrs. Sutton had said.

Finally I was in my car headed for home. But, I didn't feel like I was going home. I was leaving the only real home I had ever known. Mere weeks ago Granny deeded her house to me. She called explaining her failing health. I should've visited but work kept me away.

By the time I pulled into my parking spot at the apartment building late Tuesday evening, I had made up my mind. I had Wednesday and Thursday to pack up what little I owned so I would be ready to truly go home. There was nothing left for me here. At least in Greeneville I had Granny's house—my home. Since the apartment came furnished, I didn't have to worry about any furniture. My belongings fit into a few boxes. I used every last ounce of cleaning materials to leave the apartment spotless for the next tenant.

Late Thursday afternoon, I dropped the keys off to the landlord and started the trek back to Greeneville. I had been wandering in the desert, but I knew all along I would end up in the "Promised Land" of Granny's world—home. My body tingled all over. I had to be careful not to press on the gas too much just to arrive faster.

As HE GAZED over the hazy skyline of New York, Chase Carson wondered why he hadn't heard from Miss Olivia. She had never been tardy before. Most of the time, she would contact him weeks before her deadline to say she was ready for him to come for a visit. She didn't need him, but he needed her. He never tired of flying to East Tennessee to have some sweet tea and a chat with Miss Olivia. It was hard to believe Chase had been going to her house for almost five years. He leaned back in his chair and propped his feet on the edge of his desk. He closed his eyes and contemplated what to do.

He would find out for himself what was going on. He buzzed his assistant. "Get me a plane ticket to Greeneville."

CHAPTER TWO

DRIVING TO GRANNY Olivia's house, my mind flooded with memories of the many summers and holidays at the old house. There were those mothers who would have banned their daughter's presence because she bore a baby out of wedlock, but not Granny. She didn't approve, but she didn't punish. She forgave and then welcomed us with open arms. I enjoyed going there with my mother, but I really enjoyed the times I stayed with Granny by myself—just the two of us.

People dubbed Granny eccentric, but that was her appeal. She was unique. All who truly knew her recognized her to be a woman of strong faith who was unafraid to show it. She was independent. Though widowed early in life she had taken care of herself and her daughter. If only I could boast the same faith and independence.

I strained to catch my first glimpse of the house. As I pulled into the driveway I sat admiring the place which had always been one of safety and yet adventure. I struggled, knowing that she wouldn't be there to greet me at the front door dressed in her wild Hawaiian shirt. As soon as the door swung open, her scent accosted me. She used powder she ordered from a lady who sold Avon. It was a sweet, flowery smell. Subtle, not loud.

"Oh, what I'd do for one more slumber party, Granny."

I plopped into her favorite chair, the one with the wide armrests where she would lay her Bible and journal. What should I do now? I had a roof over my head, thanks to Granny, but I needed to find a job to keep the lights on and food in the cupboards.

Memory snapshots appeared on the album of my mind. The living room prompted a picture of the tent Granny and I made by throwing blankets across the furniture. My nose almost caught a whiff of the vanilla and maple syrup wafting from the pancakes we made in the electric skillet. Another scent drifted through my memory, the tart-buttermilk aroma of baking biscuits. Immediately my mouth watered, and I could almost taste the smooth cinnamon goodness of the apple butter that accompanied those biscuits. I wandered toward the screened-in porch and all of the sudden I was back at the picnic we had there on our magic carpet.

I wrapped my arms around myself and massaged them, hoping to lessen the ache resonating from the sheer loss. I never considered I would end up single with no plan. When I married Justin, I thought it would be forever. I was naïve or a hopeless romantic. Maybe both. Mother warned me about marrying right after high school graduation. I figured she didn't know anything about marriage. Our plan was I would work to put Justin through dental school, and then he would return the favor for me. I did my part, but I would never forget the day I caught him and Trisha. She turned out not to be a friend after all.

"We just couldn't help ourselves. We're in love," I could still hear him say.

I should've asked where I could send him a bill for all of the school I paid for and the food I put on the table. I was too hurt and angry to speak.

I scanned the kitchen. This was where I came to back then. Granny consoled me.

"It is quite difficult to procure a knight in shining armor these days," Granny had said. Her voice resonated in my head, broken with compassion. Many the world over could think of no place they might go to receive love, but I never had such a dilemma.

Suddenly my body drooped, bone-weary. A dull persistent pain pounded through the ends of my arms and legs, drawing me like a magnet to Granny's bed. I hopped the steps two at a time. Where had that needed energy burst come from?

My eyes scanned Granny's bedroom. Still unchanged. I grinned. The hardwood floors were barely visible due to the large rugs strategically placed around the room. Granny said nothing was worse than stepping from your cozy bed onto an ice-cold floor. The tall, four poster bed was still donned with the dainty floral printed comforter. The round night tables flanked each side with the antique lamps atop. Kicking off my shoes, I wiggled my toes in the soft pale pink carpet. The elaborate dresser stood at the foot of the bed. Standing in front of it, I found the brush and mirror set. Picking it up I noticed a small cluster of Granny's silver-gray hair stuck between the bristles. I swallowed at the lump in my throat.

My eyes surveyed all of the articles atop the dresser. I stopped on a framed picture and picked it up. I studied the smiling faces found there. I couldn't have been more than twelve years old. My head leaned against Granny's. Our arms were slung around each other's shoulders. Pals. I hugged the picture to my chest as if that would change the fact that Granny was gone, and I was alone.

Weariness overtook me again, and I placed the picture on the bedside table. The nearness made me feel a little less lonely.

On the small shelf across the room records still perched, ready to play a concert on the old stereo. I was convinced my granny had the idea for the first Gaither Homecoming. Every night the records would fall and ring out in succession, all the old favorites from Southern Gospel music. I pushed the button, and the first disc fell. I turned down the volume so it provided some background music in the silent house. I wasn't sure the old home could go to sleep if the concert didn't go on.

Slipping between the covers, my body sank into the pillow top, hugging me. I let out a "mmm." The bed was comfortable, but the memories even more so.

After Granny finished her Bible reading and prayer time, she would reach for her journal and entertain me with the best bedtime stories a girl could ever dream of. I jumped back out of bed just long enough to grab my journal. What a habit she had me in! People had various nighttime rituals, but Granny's was reading a little and writing a little. Now, I had her to thank for not being able to go to sleep until I had followed suit. But, I couldn't bring myself to retrieve my Bible tonight. My grudge against God still held tight.

When I opened my journal that evening, my pen hovered over the blank page. "There's nothing, Granny. I feel numb. If only I could've talked with you more."

Granny's voice echoed in my head. "Write out what you're feeling." She had told me to do that when Mom died. I had felt better afterward. Finally my hand began to move the pen across the page, spilling out every emotion in my heart. I wrote several pages, realizing the words ranged from anger to sorrow to thankfulness. By the time I had scribbled about my ire at God for taking Granny and the anguish I felt in her absence, I found myself writing memories. Granny was gone, but much too memorable to forget.

BECAUSE I HAD written well into the night, I slept in the next morning. I took my time getting ready that afternoon.

I had never been fond of funerals. I detested those who just must say something, so they announced how good the deceased looked. That comment prompted me to scream. For goodness sakes, the person was dead! Made me wonder how they looked when they were alive. I braced myself for some similar comments today. Suddenly a heavy weight gripped my chest. How would I survive this day alone? When Mom died, I had Granny right there beside me. Although she grieved, she was my fortress, she held me up. Now, I was on my own.

I moseyed to my closet in an attempt to piece together something appropriate for the funeral service. Black was such a sad color, but it has usually been the color of choice in these times. I finally located a plain dark skirt and lightweight sweater. Would the knit top work? It was nearing fall. It was all I had.

It would be best to arrive early for the funeral since I was the only living relative. Would there be questions I needed to answer? I pulled into the church parking lot at 4:15 and my eyes bulged. The lot was filled with cars. Should I return at five? Possibly there was some other activity before the funeral. I located a vacant spot, pulled in, sat, and contemplated my next move. All of the other people emerged from their cars dressed in dark colors. Could all of these people be here for Granny's funeral? As I stood, I caught a glimpse of the church sign. I looked more closely—*Miss Olivia, you will be missed.*

A new wave of sorrow rushed over me. I ambled toward the church. A line of people stretched out the entrance. I worked my way through the throng of people and was greeted by a prim and proper woman at the threshold of the sanctuary. "Do you need some assistance, my dear?" Her voice was smooth like syrup.

"I'm Alexandra Lyndon."

[109]

The woman immediately took my hand and pulled me through the crowd to the front of the church. We stopped in front of the pastor. I recognized him from the times I had visited here.

"Dear, Alexandra is here."

The minister extended his hand to me, and I placed my hand in his. "I'm so sorry for your loss. You should be here near the casket to greet others." His voice was gentle and sincere.

I released his hand and pushed through the line. My first sight of Granny brought a smile to my lips. She wore the same brightly colored Hawaiian shirt she had greeted me in that first summer I stayed with her. Why not? She had no need for mourning where she was. Black would not have been right for her. This was perfect. Although I heard people talk about how good and natural she looked, I disagreed. She was never that still. That shell had no resemblance to the woman I knew as my grandmother. After a few people began to recognize me, I had many handshakes and even hugs. People still filed into the church when the time for the funeral service arrived. The pastor asked everyone to find a seat or a spot to stand so he could proceed. I was escorted to the front pew on the right. The pastor leaned down and whispered into my ear. "Do you want to say a few words?"

A lump swelled in my throat. I swallowed hard and shook my head. I wrapped my arms around my waist and glanced at the empty pew stretching out to my right. Alone. I blinked back tears.

The minister needed no help from me anyway. He captured Granny perfectly. He obviously held her in high regard, for he struggled to keep his composure several times during his remarks. After the service, the line formed again. I was unsure how long I could endure, even though all of the sentiments rendered were heartfelt and sweet.

A warm hand grasped mine. I looked up into brilliant blue eyes. "I'm sorry for your loss." His hand lingered, holding to mine. His sandy brown hair brushed the shoulders of his blazer. "I'm Chase Carson." He smiled and studied my face. "And, you have to be Alex."

Who was this man? He knew my name. "How did you know my Granny Olivia?"

His eyes darted, and he sucked in a breath. "Business." Then, he rushed away.

CHASE SPRINTED TO his car. His pulse pounded in his ears. The pictures Miss Olivia had shown him of Alex didn't do her justice. She was petite, and he was caught off guard by her hazel eyes and dark wavy hair.

Obviously Alex had no idea about him or the reason he might be here. Miss Olivia hadn't told her granddaughter before her death. This made his mission a bit more complicated. But, he had to find what he had come to retrieve.

Would Alex have any clues? He would find out soon when he paid her a visit.

CHAPTER THREE

THE DRONING OF an engine motor wakened me. Was that a lawn mower? Not the type of alarm clock I was accustomed to. I blinked my eyes to focus. The clock over the shelf showed almost nine thirty. I almost hated waking up from my dreams, remembering Granny Olivia. Saturday had passed by in a blur of standing at the side of Granny's grave and eating a meal that the church people had insisted I attend. Exhaustion took over on Sunday, and I slept right through. Time to stop feeling sorry for myself. A growl from my stomach nearly blocked out the continual grind of the mower. I wandered toward the kitchen. Would there be something edible for breakfast? Opening the fridge, I located Granny's apple butter. What could I smear it on? I chanced a look in the freezer and spotted a bag of frozen biscuits. Jackpot! While the oven warmed, I grabbed some butter and a spoon. The buzz of the timer going off was music to my ears.

Sitting down at the small kitchen table, I thumbed through an old newspaper. Under it was a newsletter and bulletin from Grace Baptist Church, Granny's church. If I happened to be at her house on Wednesday or Sunday, Granny said we had to go church. "We mustn't forsake the gathering of the saints."

As a young girl, I had no idea what she meant, but Granny was faithful to her church and loved it. She not only said so, but she treated it as a priority.

Most of the children at the church liked Granny. She was a sucker for whatever they needed to sell for school. She would buy even if she had no use for the product, and those little tykes soon learned this. I chuckled. She had enough gift wrap stockpiled to wallpaper the entire house. She knew each child's name. Until a few years ago, Granny still did the children's sermon once a month. I still remembered how she kept not only the young ones enthralled but the whole congregation with her witty stories and clever moral lessons each Sunday morning.

"Granny, you have certainly left a big hole in many people's lives with your passing."

I had better stop poking, don some old clothes, and get to work going through some of Granny's things. That was, after all, what one did in these situations. Even though I would be living here, I wasn't sure I would do much redecorating. This place had always seemed perfect just as it was. The more I left the same, maybe the more it would feel like Granny was still here.

Stepping through the threshold of the study and den combination, I paused. This room held much magic. The three walls were still covered in shelves of books floor to ceiling. Granny said her study was the doorway into another world, because those books could take you wherever you wanted to go. There in front of the fourth wall stood her writing desk. The chair creaked as I eased into it. My mind flashed back to the many times I sat at her feet right here listening to her tell a story. A worn Bible greeted me from the desktop. I could use a cheery Psalm about now. I could open toward the middle to find the Psalms of David I craved, so I propped the book on its spine with a hand on each side and then let it fall open.

My head snapped back. "What's this?"

Instead of finding a passage from Psalms, my eyes widened to a stack of green...money. I laid it to the side and flipped to another area, again encountering money stuck between the pages. Suddenly my mind went back to what Mrs. Sutton had said. "Your inheritance is in the Word." Saying it aloud to myself made me believe what I saw. "You are quite the sly one, Granny." I giggled. Several Bibles lay nearby, each contained money, not ones and fives, but large bills. Finally I stacked the paper money together and began to count.

My mouth dropped open to discover there was a little over five hundred thousand dollars. My eyes bugged out of my head. I had never seen anywhere close to that amount of money. How had Granny gotten half a million dollars? What if someone knew about the money? What about the man from the funeral? He said he was connected to Granny through business. Maybe that's why he showed up at the funeral. My uncertainty prompted me to dress quickly and get to a bank. In this small town there were few choices. It shouldn't be difficult to choose one. As I shoved the stack of money into my purse, I was still in denial. Would the bank think I was a thief?

I strolled into the lobby of the nearby bank with my mind buzzing, contemplating how I would explain this amount of money. One look at my run-down car would have made anyone leery.

"May I help you?" a teller said.

"Yes, I need to talk to someone about opening an account."

"Just a moment."

She whirled around and returned with an older man by her side. "This is the young lady who wants to open a new account, sir."

He extended his hand toward me, and I shook it. "Right this way. I'm Mr. Davis." He led the way to a small office just off the main lobby area. "Have a seat." He waved his arm toward a chair and proceeded behind a large wooden desk. He plopped into the black leather chair and folded his hands, resting them on the desk in front of him. "Now, what can we do for you?"

"Well, I believe I need to open a savings account and maybe a small checking account so I have access to some money for needs and such."

"All right." He opened a drawer and pulled out some forms. "Now, what kind of amounts are we talking about for each? There are minimum limits on these accounts." He narrowed his gaze at me.

"I have a total of five hundred thousand dollars." I had a hard time not bursting into a fit of laughter when Mr. Davis' eyes bulged so large. I was sure he never expected such an amount to come out of my mouth.

He cleared his throat. "Well, now, I need to get your name." His pen hovered above the form, trembling a bit.

"Mr. Davis, let me back up, okay? My name is Alexandra Lyndon. My grandmother lived in the house on Main Street—Olivia Lyndon."

His expression softened. "You are Miss Olivia's granddaughter?"

"Yes, sir. Did you know her?"

"Of course. Everybody knew Miss Olivia." He smiled.

"Did she have accounts with you?"

"No." Mr. Davis laughed. I had missed the humor. "Mrs. Lyndon, your grandmother didn't believe in banks. She told me so rather apologetically on several occasions. I remember her being worried that I would think she thought me a thief. She always assured me that her feelings were nothing personal against me."

I joined him in chuckling. "That certainly sounds like her."

He studied me for a moment. "You aren't little Alex that used to come visit during the summers?"

"That's me." I nodded.

His face became serious. "I'm sorry for your loss. Truth be known, it is a loss for all of us."

"Thank you."

"Now, let's get you set up."

I left the bank feeling quite proud of my namesake. I wasn't the only one Granny Olivia had touched and made an impression upon.

A trip to the grocery store was in order. I had a plethora of canned goods, but milk and bread would be good. I also wanted some bottled water. The pipes at the old house seemed to produce a taste in an otherwise tasteless liquid. I started down the cereal aisle, not noticing anyone else until a hand touched my shoulder.

"Alexandra Lyndon?" The older woman eyed me closely.

"Yes?"

"Well, I'll be! I remember you when you were knee-high to a grasshopper." She indicated the short stature with her hand. "You and Miss Olivia came over to pick raspberries. I'm Opal." She thrust her hand toward me. Slowly my mind buzzed through memories to find a hint of recollection.

"Oh! The raspberries, yes, I do remember. How are you?"

"Old." She laughed then her expression clouded. "I do miss those days. Fun times. And, I do so miss dear Miss Olivia at our circle meeting."

I nodded in agreement. Was there anyone in this town who had not been touched by my granny? What would it be like to be like her, having a positive and lasting impact wherever I went? I could only hope to be half as effective as she had been. "It's good to see you, Opal. I'm gonna miss her, too."

I paid for the groceries and headed back toward the house. I fumbled with the bags when a strong arm took them from me. "Here, let me help you with that."

"Thanks." The man had to hear the hesitancy in my voice.

"I'm Brant Collins. Miss Olivia hired me to care for her lawn and flower beds and general maintenance."

"Oh, nice to meet you. I'm her granddaughter, Alex."

"I was wondering if you would need me to stay on and take care of the mowing and landscaping duties?"

With my inheritance safe in the bank, even if Brant knew about it, he was too late. Anyway, I had no experience in caring for a yard and definitely had no equipment. "Sure, that would be fine. I'm not sure what kind of arrangement you and my granny had."

"I normally made her an invoice of sorts. She liked to keep records."

"Fine. Thanks." I had gotten the door open. I retrieved my bags from him and closed the door with my foot. If he had ulterior motives in any way, I could keep my eyes on him.

I put away the groceries. An inventory was in order so I knew what I needed and what I didn't. There was plenty of time for that. I sighed. "God, I'm just glad I don't have to make any quick decisions for my survival."

If I played my cards right, I could just coast on the money Granny had left to me. But, I had done enough coasting in my life. I had waited for several years for my life to begin. What kind of life did I want to start? Oh, if only I had Granny here to discuss it with.

Of course, she would tell me to begin on my knees and in the Word. She would be right. Her legacy of faith was much too strong to ignore. Staying angry with God accomplished nothing. I moseyed to the study and sat down at the writing desk. This time I opened the Bible searching for another kind of wealth—answers to God's plan for my life.

MILLIE SHOWED UP at the front door early Tuesday morning. I was dressed yet somewhat disheveled. Since I only planned to putter around the house going through some other boxes, I decided no makeup or hairdo was necessary.

"I'm sorry, dear. I hope I didn't wake you."

"No, no, Millie, I've been up. Just didn't really worry about hair and makeup today. I must be a scary sight." I smoothed down my hair as best I could.

"No, you look fine. I am barging in on you unannounced anyway. I'm just so used to having tea with Olivia..." Millie bowed her head and sniffed.

My heart ached for her. She and Granny had known each other for a long time.

"You're never barging in. Come on in. I'll make us some tea."

Millie's expression brightened. She followed me into the kitchen. "Old habits are hard to break, you know? Your granny and I saw each other through the deaths of both of our husbands. We didn't allow ourselves to become lonely. We always knew the other was right next door. I think God planned it that way. Does that sound silly?"

"No, that doesn't sound silly at all." I sat down next to her, waiting for the whistle to blow on the kettle. "In fact, it sounds really great. I've never had anyone like that, you know, a real friend to share with. Except Granny."

Millie placed her hand atop mine. "Maybe you'll find someone here."

"Maybe. Hey, I wanted to ask you a question. When Granny said that my inheritance was in the Word, she really meant it. I found money stuck into all of her study Bibles. Did you know about it?"

Millie chuckled. "No, but don't that sound like her? That Granny of yours was quite the witty one. I'm not surprised." She shook her head, stirring more sugar into her tea.

"Millie, it was quite a bit of money. Where could it have come from? She didn't work anywhere, did she?"

"No, I never knew her to work, outside the home, that is. All of us women know we work hard at home. Anyway, maybe Hayward, her husband, had some kind of insurance or something when he passed. I don't know." She sipped her tea.

That could be true, but he died years ago. She could have invested the money, or my grandfather could have had a lucrative business. Still, that didn't account for the abundance of money I had found.

"By the way, what do you know about this Brant Collins guy? He says he took care of the lawn and maintenance around here."

"He's a local boy."

I forced myself not to giggle at Millie calling a grown man a boy. Of course, to a ninety-year-old woman, many people seemed like boys and girls.

"I was glad when Olivia hired him. Did you know that she did all of the yard work and maintenance herself until he came? She was amazing." She shook her head.

"I thought so too. I'm beginning to think there is a whole town full of people that have similar sentiments about Granny Olivia."

Millie stayed until we had shared two cups of tea. I loved hearing about she and Granny's visits and activities through the years.

"I better get back. Callie, my cat, will wonder where I've gotten to."

"Please feel free to come for a visit anytime. I know I'm not Granny Olivia, but I've so enjoyed spending time with you."

"Thank you, dear. That is sweet of you to say about an old wrinkled woman like me."

I walked with her to the door. Then I watched as she crossed the side yard toward her house. About halfway, she turned back and waved. I waved back and sighed. Millie and Granny must have been extremely close. The grief from the loss of her friend was painted across her face. What would it be like to have a friend like that? I had thought maybe Justin was to be my best friend. When we were first married we shared intimate talks. To have a friend so long that had shared so much of your life. That must have been special.

"Now, Alex, Jesus is my best friend. He's never too tired of hearing me talk. That's a miracle in and of itself. You just remember. Others will let you down, but Jesus never will." I could still hear Granny telling me that. At different stages in my life she said the same held true. It didn't matter if I was a young girl who had fallen off my bike or a young woman getting a divorce. She still reiterated that Jesus was the only true friend.

I moseyed back toward the study as Granny's truths swirled around in my head. I needed to check the closet. I had noticed it the day before and wondered what was kept there. As I turned the handle and pulled the door toward me, my eyes landed upon a stack of books. I picked one up and opened it. An empty journal. So this was the stockpile she drew upon when she sent me journals.

Granny Olivia always encouraged me to write. She would tell me to scribble thoughts and ideas I wanted to remember or things I observed. She told me to write stories or anything I thought should be in my book. Granny always kept many journals. In fact, she had paper every place. She said, "You never know when a thought you don't want to forget might pop up. You need something available to write it down on." She even kept a pad of paper in the bathroom. I laughed at the thought.

Granny had such wonderful stories to tell. Sometimes she would say, "I got the idea for that story standing in line at the store." Or, "I overheard a funny saying, and turned it into a tale." Or, "I couldn't go to sleep last night until I wrote down the outline for this story."

When I was a girl, I reasoned everybody had a Granny like mine who told stories. I suddenly recalled the times she felt we needed just the right atmosphere to enhance a story, so we would make a tent or use the couch for a boat. What an imagination, and how fascinating for a young girl! Oh, to get lost in another of her adventures. The real world hadn't been as kind as the world here with Granny Olivia. Maybe that was why I was here now, to get lost in a world without such struggle and disappointment. Was that possible? I wanted a different world than the one I had been living in.

As I strolled to the mailbox, I scanned my surroundings. Fall transformed the environment outside. I had not taken the time to notice, with my attention being focused on the inside of Granny's house. I had to admit, Brant had done a fine job keeping the yard looking nice. There were even new flower plantings in the beds at the front door and at the mailbox. I was sure Granny Olivia had a certain way she wanted it to be, and Brant had learned her preferences.

I skipped getting the mail and decided to go for a stroll first. The fresh air and fall-painted scenery allured me. Passing Mr. Baker's house, I wondered if he was still alive and still crabby. The next home found a couple seated on the porch in their swing. They waved to me as I strolled by, and I returned the greeting. Coming to Opal's house, I questioned if her raspberry bushes still produced berries after the summer I ate most of them.

The birds' song mixed with the scenery like a museum with a background cantata. In this neighborhood God had slowed time for people to enjoy His creation and His presence. What a contrast from the hustle-bustle of my life in Knoxville. At the end of the street an older man looked on as a young boy rode a small bike in the driveway. His old car was parked along the curb, no doubt giving the little guy more room to practice. Obviously the boy was just learning to perfect riding a bicycle, for the man shouted encouragement from the sidelines.

"You're getting it now, Johnny!"

The small boy's face was covered with a smile, and he sat tall with pride.

What had I missed? My life had been a series of starts with no finishes. No husband, no family, no children, no career. I gazed up past the rustling leaves to the clear blue sky beyond. I had nothing.

"You always have Jesus."

The words were so clear, I turned to look behind me, fully expecting to see Granny there beside me on the sidewalk. No Granny, but the sun twinkled through the foliage of the trees making jewels on the concrete walk. I sighed. I was glad I still heard Granny's wisdom reverberating around me. I hummed a familiar tune. My eyes misted over when I realized the song was 'Jesus Loves Me'. Finally back at the house, I almost forgot the mail. Halfway up the walkway, I turned around.

I was unsure what kind of mail Granny would receive, if any. However, if there were correspondences, I needed to send word of her passing. There were three envelopes. Two were clearly junk, since they were marked for current resident. The third envelope intrigued me. The name Olivia Lyndon showed through the plastic window. The page inside had a background like a check. I carried it inside and opened it. It was a check from a publishing company in New York. The memo line read—Alexa Livingston.

Now I was really confused. I paused in the entry a moment. My mother had explained that my name, Alexandra, came from Granny Olivia. Her middle name was Alexa if I remembered correctly, but Livingston wasn't right. Lyndon was her last name. I wandered into the study, searching the desk for a clue as to whether this actually belonged to Granny or not and why she would receive it. In the left-hand drawer of the desk there was a book—different than a journal. Upon opening it, it appeared to be some kind of ledger. So she did keep some kind of records, even though she didn't trust a bank. I chuckled. I scanned the pages and found entries from the Carson Publishing Company, which matched the name on the check I found in the mailbox. Well, it must have come to the right place, but what was it for? I turned to the first page of the ledger and sure enough, there was the matching name—Alexa Livingston. Was that Granny's maiden name? Why would she receive a correspondence with her middle and maiden names on it? And, why did she receive a check from a publishing company? I replaced the book and scanned the check and accompanying invoice again. Aha! A phone number and contact name.

I was hesitant at first, because I had no idea who I was calling or exactly what to say. I also wasn't sure that anyone would still be at the number this late in the evening. But, I had to know what to do with the check. It was made out for a substantial amount—ten thousand dollars! I picked up my cell phone before I lost my courage. I spotted the signature on the check and froze, putting my phone aside. Chase Carson—the man from the funeral.

CHAPTER FOUR

THE SUN WAS glowing over the mountain ridge that Wednesday morning when Chase knocked at Miss Olivia's front door. He had tried to give Alex Lyndon time to grieve, but he had to get this settled. He still practiced what he was going to say, because he was unsure how to approach the reason for his visit. The door flew open. Miss Olivia's granddaughter froze, wide-eyed.

"It's you." Her eyes narrowed as she studied him.

"Chase Carson." He stuck his hand toward her. She fumbled and finally shook it. "You are Alex, right? Miss Olivia's granddaughter?"

"Uh, yes. I'm glad to see you again because I have some questions about a letter. Please come in." She kept her eyes on Chase as he brushed by her. She closed the door and gestured toward the sofa. "Please have a seat."

Alex plunked down in a chair across from him and scrutinized him for a long moment. The silence became uncomfortable—it edged on embarrassing. Finally, he shook his head slightly to clear it or bring it into focus.

"I'm sorry to hear about Mrs. Livingston, I mean, Mrs. Lyndon."

"Thank you. I'm still not used to the idea that she is gone." She fingered the arm of the chair, and her shoulders drooped.

"And you say you are her granddaughter. Is that right?" Chase couldn't be wrong about her identity. He couldn't afford to tell the wrong person.

"Yes." Her tone held an edgy or offensive overture. Had his question sounded as if he didn't believe who she was?

He cleared his throat. "I don't mean to offend. It's just that I must make sure who you are before I divulge what I will."

Her brow wrinkled, and she leaned forward, crossing her arms over her chest. She glanced around the room. "Am I being filmed for some reality show? Those shows where they reveal some secret or long lost loved one and then record the person's reaction?"

Chase stifled a chuckle.

"Look, I don't know what this is all about, but I am Alexandra Lyndon. I am the daughter of my Granny Olivia's only daughter, who is also gone. I just want to know what is going on." Her voice had a desperate tone, and her hands trembled.

He sighed and smiled at her. "I didn't come here to upset you. I would never want to do that. Miss Olivia wanted you to know after her death, but no one else."

Alex rubbed her arms as if a chilly wind had just blown through the room. "Know what?" Her voice shook.

"The letter you received was her royalty check. Your granny was an author. A very popular one at that."

Her hands dropped to her lap, and her eyes widened. "An author?"

"Yes, she wrote Christian novels—romance and mystery."

"Why did I never know?"

"She didn't want anyone to know. At first she used her pen name so she could keep her privacy. Then she also realized over the last few years that her readers might not be as excited about reading romance from a ninety-year-old woman." He chuckled.

She fell back into the chair, shook her head, and laughed.

Chase was puzzled by her reaction.

"Thank goodness. I thought she might have been involved in something illegal or something. That explains all of the money she left me. Wow, I should've figured that out." She shook her head again.

Chase listed some of Miss Olivia's titles. Alex nodded. "I've read some of them myself. I should have recognized her writing. I've heard it all my life."

Chase became serious again and leaned forward, looking into her eyes. "Here's the problem. There's one last manuscript that ends the series. I know it was complete because she told me. I just have no idea where it is. There are quite a few people who would like to get their hands on it. It is worth a lot of money. The readers are waiting for it. It should be a CD. She always wrote in long hand and then a typist put it on a disk for her."

She scratched her head. "I haven't run across it yet. I've been trying to go through some of Granny's things. I don't plan to change much though. This place has always been perfect just the way it is." Alex scanned the room and then gazed back at him. "Do you have any ideas where to look?"

"I was hoping you would have some ideas."

"Well, there is the reading of the will on Thursday. From what the lawyer said there's not much there, but maybe there would be something. A clue?" She shrugged. "You're welcome to come with me." Pink shot to her cheeks. "I mean…you can attend."

"Thank you for the invitation. I think I'll take you up on that." He rubbed the stubble on his chin. Would he be too forward to ask to pick her up? The idea made sense—they were going to the same place. "Umm, could I offer to drive you?"

Alex diverted her eyes from his gaze. Her cheeks were now red. "If that's not any trouble?" Her gaze met his again, brows raised.

Chase's heart pounded a little harder. She was cute even though she wore work clothes and her hair was pulled back. "No trouble," his voice squeaked out.

THE NEXT MORNING his pulse doubled once again when she emerged from the front door. Her dark wavy hair hung down past her shoulders, making her hazel eyes sparkle. When she flashed a smile, an adorable dimple appeared on her right cheek. He motioned toward the car, not trusting his voice at the moment. As he followed her down the sidewalk, he noticed how her knee-length dress hugged her thin waist. What was he doing?

He slid into the driver's seat, catching a whiff of vanilla. He needed to focus.

"I really appreciate you taking me to the reading of the will. I'm a little nervous. I've never had to do anything like this before. I'm afraid Granny Olivia was always the one I could count on to be at my side. Now that she's gone..." Her voice trailed off, and she stared out the windshield.

Chase's chest tightened, knowing what losing a loved one was like. "I'm glad I can go with you." Their eyes met for a split second. There went his heart again.

There was no discussion except for Alex's directions as she told him where the lawyer's office was located. He pulled into a parking spot. "Ready?"

She bit her bottom lip, met his gaze, and nodded.

He followed behind Alex, led by the lawyer into the conference room, which was cold and nondescript with an oblong table and accompanying chairs. An older woman rose to greet Alex. Upon sitting down, he spied a man seated across the table. Who could these people be? As far as he knew Miss Olivia had only one relative and that was Alex. The man appeared rather cross, instead of mournful with his wrinkled brow and set jaw. Alex stared momentarily at the man with wide eyes and semi-slack jaw. Was she confused or surprised by his presence, too?

The lawyer cleared her throat like a signal to begin, although there was really no need, for the room was already silent.

"Good morning. I am Mrs. Sutton. I will be reading aloud a letter in Mrs. Lyndon's own hand." She held up a sheet of stationery. "She insisted on writing an informal will of sorts in this manner."

"Dearest Alex, you are the only daughter of my only daughter. Who could have believed that she would go home before me? Yet, cancer can be a mighty opponent, and God has His plan for us all. You, Alex, have been most precious to me." A sob escaped from Alex. "You will find my final words and your inheritance all in the Word. Use it wisely. Keep your journals. Don't give up on love. Welcome those things God brings into your path. Until I meet you on the other side, take care and know I love you. It is signed, Granny Olivia." Mrs. Sutton glanced at Alex.

Tears streamed down Alex's cheeks. The lawyer pushed a box of tissues across the table. Alex snatched two and dabbed her face.

"There's a P.S. here. For my dear and longtime friend Millie, please take the tea set. We have shared many tea times around that old tea pot. It belongs to you." The lawyer nodded toward the older lady. "For Brant, who has faithfully served me, I want you to have the small coin collection. I know you have an interest in that area."

"That's it?" The man across the table let out a heavy sigh.

Alex glared at him. "What were you expecting?"

He rolled his eyes as if he had no time for idle chat. "I just thought...it doesn't matter."

"I am her only living relative, her granddaughter, Alexandra Lyndon." She leaned forward in an almost challenging stance. She sucked in a breath and turned toward Mrs. Sutton. "Thank you for your time. Could I have the letter?"

"Yes, of course. Your grandmother insisted on writing it herself. She kept saying it was important to get it right. I'm not sure why."

Alex reached for the letter and handled it as if it were a million dollars, hugging it to her chest. "Sounds like her."

"What did she mean exactly about your inheritance being in the Word?" Mrs. Sutton leaned forward, brows knitted.

Alex paused and grinned. "You obviously didn't know her very well, as I suspect of others." She glanced across the table at Brant and then back to the lawyer. "My grandmother was a Christian woman who was strong in her faith. To her, the instructions from the Word of God, the Bible, are a precious inheritance. But, her life was proof enough." She stared at the letter again.

The older woman patted Alex's arm then the two enfolded each other in an embrace. They pushed back both drying tears with a tissue. "Honey, are you all right?"

"I think so."

"Of course, she had already deeded the house and its contents to you months before her death. So, I guess that's it." The lawyer shrugged.

"Thank you again."

Chase offered his arm to Alex, and she wrapped her dainty hand around it. They walked in silence to the car. He helped her into the passenger seat and then jogged around to the driver's side and hopped in.

"I'm sorry this wasn't any help in finding the manuscript."

"That's okay. It was a longshot." He angled his body toward her. "I really am sorry for your loss."

"Thank you. I feel so guilty." Her lower lip quivered. "Granny had requested I come for a visit when she deeded the house, but I just couldn't get away. I was foolish. I should've made more of an effort. I would've had more time with her." She sniffed.

"Don't beat yourself up. Do we ever show our loved ones enough of how special they are to us? I don't think so."

"I guess you're right."

"Who were the other two people in there if you are the only family?"

"The older woman is Millie. She has been Granny Olivia's neighbor and friend since before I can remember. Now she'll be my neighbor. I don't want to neglect her. Granny wouldn't approve of that." She swiped her nose with a tissue. "The man was Brant. I just met him. He takes care of the yard and maintenance duties. I'm not sure why he was there, or that I should've agreed to keep him on."

"Let's get you home. You've had a rough couple of days."

Chase pulled into the driveway of Alex's house and put the car in park. "Do you need a few days? I can make myself scarce."

"No, we need to continue to look for that manuscript. I know you're eager to find it and go home."

Not that eager to go home anymore. "Do you have any ideas?"

"Well, I do know Granny Olivia didn't trust a bank for her money, but the man that opened my account sure knew her pretty well. I never asked if maybe she had a safety deposit box or something."

"Sounds like a good place to begin. How about I pick you up about nine in the morning? We can check it out."

"Okay." Her voice was low.

"Look, you have to know that Miss Olivia was more than a client of mine. I didn't need to come all the way here from New York to pick up her manuscripts, but I did. She was a great lady." His voice broke, and he cleared his throat to regain his composure.

"Thank you for saying that. I'm glad you told me. I guess I wondered if it was all about finding the book for the money." She diverted her gaze to her lap.

"No. But, that book deserves to be found and published. It's only fitting the end of her story be told. You know what I mean?"

She looked at him and nodded. "I think I do."

"You do know that all of the royalties will divert to you, right?"

"Really?" She bit her bottom lip.

"That's the way she wanted it."

She shifted in the seat. "So, she told you about me?"

"Sure. She was quite fond of you. She used to tell me stories." He stroked his chin, grinning.

"Oh, no! I'm not sure I want to know." She feigned covering her ears and shaking her head.

They both laughed. Chase escorted her to the front door. "I'm glad I'm getting the opportunity to meet you."

Her face reddened. "See you in the morning."

Chase resisted the urge to kiss her.

I PEEKED OUT the curtains, watching Chase pull away. What a couple of days this had been!

The evening was still early, but my lack of sleep the night before was catching up to me fast. I stumbled up the stairs into the bedroom. As I completed my Bible reading and journal writing, I fell back onto the pillow. My mind still reeled from all that I had learned. Granny Olivia, an author. Not just any author, but a famous one. But, no one knew who she was except me...and Chase.

"And, what kind of things did you tell Chase anyway?" I said toward the picture of Granny and me on the bedside table. "You were always one to be full of surprises."

CHAPTER FIVE

WHEN CHASE ARRIVED at the hotel, he plopped onto the bed with a heavy sigh. He experienced some degree of shock over Miss Olivia's death. He still couldn't believe she was gone. Her fans would miss her books, but he would miss the woman. There would never again be a need to come to East Tennessee to retrieve her latest manuscript. His shoulders drooped and his heart ached with the realization. He lay back on the bed. Every trip had become like an oasis in the busyness that was his life.

A smile crept to his face as he visualized Alex with her petite form and dark wavy hair. Her olive green eyes sported copper flecks and were hard to look away from, and he adored the dimple on her right cheek when she smiled. He hadn't expected to find Miss Olivia's granddaughter, nor had he anticipated to discover her so alluring. He felt himself rather rude to even think about her that way at this time, just after losing her granny, as she called her. He couldn't help himself. She filled his thoughts no matter what else he tried to concentrate on. Finally, he focused long enough to call his mother. She would want to know about Miss Olivia.

"Hello? Son?"

"Yes, it's Chase, Mom. Everything okay there?" He sat up, leaning his back on the bed's headboard.

"Oh, yes. How about with you?"

"I had to make a quick trip to Tennessee. I have some bad news." He ran his fingers through his hair.

"What is it?"

"Miss Olivia died."

"Oh, son." Chase could hear his mother's voice crack and some sniffing.

"I know. I'm still in shock myself. I never really wanted to think about this day coming, but she was ninety." He leaned his head back.

"What a godly woman. She will be missed."

"She already is. By the way, I'm going to make sure everything is okay at the office first, but I plan to stay on a few days." He stood and walked to his suitcase.

"Why?"

"Well, there's a bit of mystery going on here for Alex and me." He shuffled through his clothes until he found his sleep shorts.

"Who's Alex?"

"Oh, she's Miss Olivia's granddaughter."

"Mmm, really?"

He rolled his eyes at her intrigued tone. "Mom! She didn't even know that her granny, that's what she called her, was an author."

"Really?"

"Yeah, Miss Olivia kept her secret from everyone. When she said it was all about touching lives and not her fame, she really meant it." He plopped into a chair, sliding his feet out of his shoes.

"So, tell me more about this Alex."

Chase's face became hot. His hesitance must have cued his mother to the fact that he had some kind of feelings toward Alex. "You still there?"

"Yes, Mom." Chase winced and shook his head, reprimanding himself when his voice cracked.

"Is she that attractive?" She giggled.

"I just met her."

"She has certainly made an impression on you quickly for you to be at such a loss for words."

Chase could hear the smile in her voice. He visualized her eyes probing his for information. "Well, if you must know, yes, Alex is rather attractive. But, the big mystery now is where Miss Olivia's latest manuscript is. I'm going to pick Alex up in the morning to begin the search." He welcomed the mystery, because it gave him a reason to stay and see Alex again.

"Keep me informed on all of the mystery. Oh, and Chase, wear something nice tomorrow. Maybe blue to compliment your eyes."

"Mom!" Chase heaved a heavy sigh. "I gotta go. Love you."

She was giggling as she hung up the phone. The heat had yet to leave his face. He stood up and moseyed to the closet, hoping to find a blue shirt.

THE NEXT MORNING I awakened more refreshed after actually sleeping instead of fretting throughout the night. Hopefully that would help the bags under my eyes to have lessened. This morning I needed to take a little more care in my appearance. Not that I was trying to impress anyone, but I didn't want to look like something the cat dragged in. Amazing how those little sayings popped right into my head because I often heard them growing up. Granny had all kinds of statements that regularly emitted from my mother's mouth and now mine.

After showering, I took some extra time with my hair and makeup. I searched until I found my best jeans and a short-sleeve sweater my mother always said flattered my figure. As I stopped for one last look at myself in the bedroom dresser mirror, I laughed at myself. It had been so long since I had any interaction with a man. Not that I was trying to cause anything to happen. I just didn't want to appear homely. Mr. Chase Carson lived in big New York City and encountered lots of sophisticated people. I didn't want him to return confirming what was said about us Tennesseans—that we walked around with no shoes and wore overalls. I laughed again at my reflection. Who was I trying to fool? Chase was an attractive and successful man. Who was I? Divorced. Unemployed. Stuck in limbo.

There was the knock and right on time. I scurried to the door. I stopped and took a deep breath, trying not to appear so eager. I eased the door open. "Morning."

Chase did a double take. "Morning. Um...did you sleep well?"

"Much better last night with some of the mystery about Granny answered."

"Good, then I guess we'll be on our way." He flashed a perfect smile.

I gave him directions to the bank I had set up accounts in. I figured it would be as good of a place to start as any. Upon entering the bank, Mr. Davis spotted me right away. When a person deposited half a million dollars, people remembered.

"Miss Lyndon, what a pleasure. How can I help you today?"

"Well, Mr. Davis, I wonder if we might step into your office so I can ask you a question."

Mr. Davis eyed Chase suspiciously.

"Oh, I'm sorry. He's with me. This is Chase Carson."

The two men shook hands. Then we followed the bank manager into his office. After we were seated, I began. "I know you told me the other day that Granny Olivia never trusted putting her money in a bank. But I wondered if she might have had a safety deposit box for other valuables?"

Mr. Davis clucked his tongue and shook his head. "I'm afraid not. As I said, she would tell all bankers or financial-types that she apologized for her distrusting manner. She always said it was nothing personal." He shrugged and grinned, folding his hands onto his desk.

"Thank you for your time." Chase started to stand but stopped.

"Have you lost something?" Mr. Davis leaned forward, brows raised.

"Not exactly. I believe there is more to my inheritance."

"More money?" Mr. Davis' eyes bulged.

"No, it is something else. But, thank you."

Chase rose to exit.

"If there is anything else I can do for you, don't hesitate to call."

I nodded at the bank manager. "Oh, actually, I was planning to deposit another check in my savings account, but I'll just take care of that with one of your tellers."

Mr. Davis jumped to his feet. "No need. I can take care of that for you."

I suppressed a chuckle at his flighty manner.

When we were back in Chase's rental car, I let out a heavy sigh.

"I would've loved to have been there when you opened that account with him. I'm surprised he didn't pass out."

I leaned my head on the headrest and laughed. "He was quite excited that I wasn't like my grandmother and kept my money myself."

"Now what?"

I turned in the seat to face him. "I suppose we could ask around the neighborhood. I have found since I've been here everyone knew and loved Granny Olivia. Maybe we could get some kind of clue."

"Okay."

"The best place to start would be Millie, the next door neighbor. She and Granny were close friends."

"The lady from the will reading?"

I nodded.

Chase started the engine, and we headed back toward the house.

Millie immediately invited us in, and I made the introductions. I made a quick explanation of Chase's connection with Granny Olivia. "Millie, we are looking for a final manuscript that Mr. Carson knows is complete. We know she didn't have anything in the bank."

"Oh, no, she would never put a thing in any bank. You're right about that." Mille studied her folded hands for a moment. "The only other place she frequented was the church. She was devoted to her church."

I looked to Chase. "I don't think she would hide a manuscript at the church, but we might get some kind of hint or clue if we visit there. We could talk to the pastor."

We said our goodbyes and headed back to the car. Before Chase left the curb, he turned toward me. "By the way, it's Chase, not Mr. Carson." His eyes looked warm and the deep blue color seemed to sparkle.

My face heated, and I could only nod.

We found the pastor in his study. "Dear Miss Olivia, I miss her already. She always encouraged me, and that is few and far between for a minister."

"We are just trying to solve this mystery of the missing manuscript. I'm sure it's not here, but we thought maybe something you might say would give us something to go on." I scooted to the edge of my chair.

"Well, all I can say is she called me just two weeks before her death and asked if I would come for a visit. I went right over. She discussed her funeral arrangements for a few moments and then she handed me an envelope." The pastor smiled and shook his head. "She laughed and indicated that was her tithe for the next few years. I didn't open it until I arrived back at the church. It was a substantial amount of money. But, I wasn't really surprised. She was always meeting needs for the people of our church. She gave several scholarships for youth trips, and when she heard there was someone in need, she was always there to provide. She was faithful right up until those last few weeks. She was active in the senior group and especially the Women's Missionary Union. She was...a precious saint."

"I know. The more I hear about her, the more I wished I had gotten to know her even better," Chase said.

As each person spoke fondly of Granny, I became prouder, and yet there was a degree of sadness. I was wishing the same thing Chase was, that I had been around during this last phase of her life so I would have known her better. "Thank you."

I slumped into the car with a heavy sigh.

"This is hard on you. I'm sorry." Chase's tone sounded so sincere.

I looked again into Chase's eyes. As his mouthed curled up into a pleasant smile, little crinkles appeared at the corner of his lids. I could certainly get lost in those baby blues if I allowed myself. But, that would never happen. He was just being kind because of the situation. "I guess we go back to the house and search some more." I shrugged.

We rode in silence. This was indeed hard. With all of the scurrying around, my grieving had been put on hold. Yet my heart seemed hollow and my chest ached.

Upon entering the house, I turned to Chase.

"Where do we start?" Chase asked.

"We can continue in the study, which is where I found some important papers. I keep thinking maybe there is a safe or a metal box somewhere that might contain the manuscript."

Chase placed his hands on my shoulders and looked into my eyes. His touch sent tingles down my back. "It's enough for today. Go take a bubble bath or something. Go to bed early and try to rest. I'll see you in the morning. Okay?"

I nodded wearily. I was relieved. I truly wondered how I would find the motivation to start searching the house in my present state. Actually a bath and a good cry would be welcome.

CHAPTER SIX

SHEER EXHAUSTION MUST have been the reason I slept through the night and awakened more refreshed than I thought possible. When Chase arrived I steered him toward the kitchen where I had hot biscuits ready with Granny's apple butter on the side.

"Ooo, something smells good." His eyes danced.

"That's the biscuits, but it's the apple butter that will keep you coming back."

He wiggled his eyebrows.

My stomach fluttered. "Just eat your biscuit."

"Mmm, you're right." He lifted the jar turning it around, searching. "What kind is this?"

"Granny's homemade." I grinned.

"You're kidding me. What all did that woman do?"

"You'd be surprised."

We savored in silence.

"I thought we might start in the bedroom closet. I haven't looked there at all yet."

"Okay. Lead on." He bowed slightly and swept his arm forward.

We discovered several shoe boxes with lids in the top of Granny's closet. Chase handed me the boxes one by one, and I placed them on the bed. Then I hopped up in the middle of them all and opened the first one. It was full of envelopes. I pulled one out and removed the letter inside.

Dear Mother,

Please pray for me as I brave this new experience. Robert made it quite clear that his only involvement with the baby would be to help me get rid of it. The thought made me sick to my stomach. I told him I never wanted to lay eyes on anyone that could even think of doing anything to harm a precious child. He obliged. I am sorry for any embarrassment or shame this might bring upon you. Thank you for not turning me away when I visited to tell you of the pregnancy. I will try to visit soon. Pray for a healthy baby. Pray for me to be a good mother.

I love you,
Michelle

I hugged the letter to my chest.

"What is it? Your face is pale." Chase sat on the side of the bed, looking at me intently. "Do you feel all right?" He rubbed my arm.

I handed the page to him. "This letter is from my mother to my Granny. It's about me."

"Are you sure you want me to read it?'

I nodded and dug into the box for another letter.

Dear Mother,

Alexandra is growing so fast. I can't wait to bring her again to visit. You will not believe how alert she is. I'm so happy she looks like you and me. I'm not sure she will be happy with that fact. When she coos, my heart sings. I cannot describe it, yet you are a mother, I suppose you understand. Trying to work and go to nursing school with a baby is grueling, but I know I would have it no other way. I received some more scholarship money today. I wanted to tell you so you wouldn't worry. God has taken care of me through this scholarship. My babysitter is a wonderful woman from the church. She adores Alex. I do long for the time when I can be with her more, to have school behind me. Patience is not something I have a lot of. Continue to pray that I will be a good mother just as you were and always are to me.

With much love,
Michelle and Alex

"I had no idea what a struggle it was for her when I was a baby. By the time I was old enough to know, she made it look so simple." I shrugged.

"I didn't know." Chase's voice was low and full of emotion.

"I wasn't sure how much you knew about me."

"Not as much as I'd like to." He leaned my way, bumping his shoulder against mine.

I grinned.

"Now, there's some color in your cheeks."

I shoved his arm. "I'm sorry. This isn't helping your quest for the manuscript."

He placed his hand lightly on my arm. "We'll find that. I think you need this." He indicated the letters.

"Thank you. I think I do."

Each letter described what new milestone I had reached whether it was walking or talking. The next box held letters and copies of some sort. Upon closer inspection, the papers discussed the scholarship my mother mentioned getting for her nursing school. There were money order stubs signed by Granny. A letter at the bottom of the box explained more fully what we had found.

Dear Mr. Cunningham,

Enclosed you will find the funds for Michelle Lyndon's nursing school this semester. The enclosed document is for her. Please do not reveal the donor of this money for I prefer to do this anonymously. Thank you for your cooperation in this matter.

Sincerely,

Olivia Lyndon

I placed my hand over my opened mouth.

"What have you discovered now?" Chase eyed the documents I held.

"Granny paid for Mother's schooling under the guise of a scholarship. I bet my mother never knew."

"Wow, your grandmother was quite a woman."

The next box was full of pictures of a very young Granny Olivia.

Chase pointed toward the photo in my hand.

"Who's the guy?"

I studied it more closely. "I guess that must be Granny's husband, Hayward. She didn't speak of him very much. She was widowed quite early in their marriage."

We sorted through pictures, even finding one that must have been the day the two were married. On the very bottom were a death certificate, obituary, and a newspaper article. "This death certificate lists cause of death as accidental, but look at this article."

Chase scanned the article and then looked wide-eyed at me. "This states that your grandfather was found dead at his office desk with some type of pills nearby. It was thought to have been accidental death because it was assumed he took too many of the pills."

I crossed my arms. "Yes, but did you read the part about Granny Olivia? The reporter quotes Granny as saying there was no way it was accidental. She felt he had been murdered. Something about a jealous partner."

Chase's eyes widened, and he snapped his finger. "Oh, wait. This is in one of her books. *The Lone Survivor* has this scenario in it."

"Really? I haven't read that one. The things she lived with during her lifetime. She was stronger than I ever realized."

Before I knew it, we had spent the whole day going through shoe boxes. I asked Chase to replace them in the closet. Those were treasures I couldn't dispose of. It seemed Granny kept just about everything, but I was glad. I was beginning to piece together the story of her life and even parts of my mother's. Parts I would've never known otherwise.

I walked Chase to the door. His shoulders slumped in a defeated manner. "I'm sorry. I know we made no headway on what we are really trying to find. But..."

He put a finger to my lips to stop me. "I'm not sorry. I could see how important finding those things was for you. I would never take that away from you—not for thirty manuscripts."

"We can try again tomorrow. I've only scratched the surface in the study. We'll start there."

Chase tilted his head, eyeing me. "Do I get more apple butter and biscuits?"

I tapped my chin with my finger and pursed my lips. "Umm, unless you like pancakes?"

Chase's face lit up. "I'll be here at eight!"

I chuckled. "Okay."

I closed the door behind him and sighed. I was beginning to really enjoy his company.

CHAPTER SEVEN

I FLIPPED OFF the downstairs lights mindlessly. My mind was on where else we might search for that manuscript. Admittedly, I was glad we had discovered the boxes today. The letters and pictures cleared up many questions I had about my mother and Granny. Of course, there were other things I would have never thought to ask but was revealed in those letters and documents.

As I settled between the covers of the bed, I relished in the idea that I knew my mother and grandmother a little better. I was truly proud to be a Lyndon woman. I could only hope to live a life with as much care and influence. Would God give me that opportunity? To be someone who made a difference?

I woke to a noise downstairs. Still, the house remained dark. The glowing hands on my clock showed 2:30. Was I only dreaming? Was that why I awakened? I turned over and began to settle in to drift off to sleep again when a loud echo sounded from the first floor. Goosebumps spread up my arms. Someone was in the house. I rose from the bed, being careful to avoid the place I had learned creaked. I scanned the room for some kind of weapon. A vase perched on a small shelf near the record player. I tiptoed over and lifted it slowly. I stepped into the hallway and froze. There was definitely someone walking around on the first floor. Not knowing the location of the creaks in the wooden floor boards, the intruder stepped on each one. My heart pounded so hard I was surprised I heard anything.

The vase began to tremble in my grasp. I steadied it with my other hand. I eased to the top of the stairs and looked down into the dark. All that could be seen were shadows due to the neighborhood lights shining in from outside. Suddenly, a shadow darted in front of the steps below. I gasped and the figure turned toward me. Upon noticing me there at the top of the stairs, the figure spun around and sprinted for the exit. I scurried down the steps in time to see the retreating form rush out the front door and into the night, leaving the door wide open. I ran to the door, slammed it shut, and locked it. I eased the vase down on the entry table. I feared in my violent shaking, I might drop it. I bolted up the stairs and dialed Chase's cell number before I thought about the time.

"Hello?" His voice was groggy and barely audible.

"Chase, it's Alex. Someone was in the house." I wrapped my arm around my waist.

"Are you all right? Is the person gone?"

"I saw him flee out the front door. I'm really shaken, but I'm okay." I worked to slow my breathing.

"I'm on my way."

"No, I hate that I called you at this time of night. I dialed before I thought."

"Good, I'm glad. I'll be right there."

I immediately flew to the living room to wait for Chase. Every noise jolted my nerves. I sat still glancing around the room, looking for any movement. My breath caught in my throat when a knock sounded from the front door. I sprinted to the entry and paused, listening.

"It's me." Chase's familiar voice seeped through the door, reaching me with welcomed relief.

I jerked open the door and fell into his arms. He embraced me and eased me inside, closing the door behind us. He led me to the couch and sat down still holding me. He placed his hands around my face and looked into my eyes. "Are you okay?"

I nodded, but tears slid down my cheeks. He pulled me close again. His hand smoothed my hair gently. My tension released slowly. I buried my face in his shoulder and let the fear drain through the tears. Reluctantly, I pulled away, swiping at my wet cheeks with the back of my hand.

Chase looked me in the eyes. "We should call the police."

Despite the situation, his gaze melted me.

"Chase, I don't know what we'll say. There's nothing missing—not even valuables that were in plain sight. He was looking for something, and I startled him before he found it."

"Him—it was a man?"

"I can't say for sure because I only saw a shadow. I guess I say 'he' because the build and height seemed more like a man than a woman." We still sat close, our legs touching.

"Well, it's too early for pancakes." He glanced around the room. "Do you have an extra blanket?"

"Why?"

"Because I'm sleeping right here." He indicated the couch.

I shook my head. "No, I can't ask you to do that."

He caught my hands and squeezed. "You didn't ask me. I'm doing it. I can't leave you here alone."

Fetching a blanket gave me a good excuse to leave the room and regain my composure. If I didn't move away, Chase would surely detect my strong attraction to him. I sprinted up the stairs and returned with one of Granny's quilts and a pillow.

"Thanks." He touched my cheek again.

"You're welcome."

His gaze and hand lingered a moment, bringing a peace to my body. I closed my eyes momentarily and his lips lightly brushed mine. My whole body tingled at his touch and kiss. My eyes flew open. His expression was soft, and his eyes intense with concern. "Try to sleep a little more. Go ahead." He directed me to the steps, and I meandered to the bedroom.

As I settled between the covers once again, I smiled. As I closed my eyes, I hoped he had experienced the same feeling I had during that intimate moment. If not, I was on a course to make a fool of myself.

About eight the next morning I decided to give up on sleeping. Between the break-in incident and the fact that Chase was asleep just downstairs, I couldn't seem to doze off again for very long. I donned some sweats, ran a brush through my hair, and dabbed at the dark circles under my eyes with some makeup powder. Then I eased down the stairs and peeked toward the living room. Chase was lying on his back. I watched the rise and fall of his chest under the blanket. His lashes lay feathery against his cheek. I couldn't deny he was an attractive man in looks as well as personality. But, what did I have to offer him in return? He was way out of my league.

I tiptoed to the kitchen to begin preparing pancake batter as I had promised. Chase deserved a hearty breakfast even more for running to me in the middle of the night and then camping out on the couch. As I flipped the first pancake over on the griddle, Chase trudged around the corner, nose in the air sniffing. His hair was mussed and his chin covered with a shadow made of stubble. Even in his disheveled appearance, he was beautiful. Is this what it would be like...? I bit my lip to stop that train of thought.

"Morning. Thanks again for staying last night. I know that couch was probably not as comfortable as your hotel bed."

"I could've never gotten comfortable back at the hotel knowing you were here alone." He looked over my shoulder. "Mmm, that smells good. What should I do?"

I nodded my head toward the table. "Just sit down. These are ready."

I scooped off a stack from the griddle and placed them in front of him. In minutes I had a matching stack. I sat down across from him and began to slather my pancakes in butter and syrup. The first bite filled my mouth with sweet maple warmth.

Chase licked his lips. "These are so good."

"I'm glad."

He set his fork down intentionally and looked straight at me. "Are you okay?"

"Yeah, I think so." I took a gulp of milk. "I can't lie. Having an uninvited intruder in the house is unnerving." And, having Chase near was unnerving in a different way.

"I can imagine." He sighed.

Suddenly, a thought occurred to me. "Do you think they were after the manuscript?"

"I don't know. Miss Olivia's books made quite a bit of money, as you have discovered. The only reason I would suspect that he was after the book is because there were valuables, as you said, in plain sight that were untouched. That lets me know he wasn't just some thief looking for items to steal and sell."

"He obviously didn't find what he was looking for. I just hope he doesn't come back." I shuddered at the thought.

He pointed his fork at me. "Until we make sure he isn't coming back, I won't let you stay here alone."

"Oh, Chase, I'm sure I'll be fine." I forced a smile, trying to reassure him or maybe myself.

"I'm sure you will be too with me camping on your couch." He gave me an emphatic nod.

"I'm gonna get this cleaned up, and then we can nose around the study." I stood, collecting our plates.

"Here, let me help." He jumped up, scooping up the silverware and glasses.

"You don't have to do that."

"I know, but I want to. You made these wonderful pancakes. The least I can do is help you clean up the mess." He proceeded to roll up his sleeves in a dramatic manner.

I laughed. I washed and he dried. The task took a little longer because Chase had me laughing about his inadequacies when it came to cooking.

"Growing up my mother would never let me help do anything except dry dishes. When I got out on my own, I couldn't even make toast. Trust me when I say the whole apartment building knew when I tried. I set off the fire alarms regularly."

"How about now?" I stifled a giggle.

"Let's just say I thank the good Lord for all of the one skillet meals available these days. I can make those without summoning the local fire department."

I stacked the last utensil in the drawer. Chase draped the drying towel over the side of the counter and ran his fingers through his hair.

"I think I'll run to my hotel and grab a quick shower. Be back in thirty. You'll be all right?"

"Of course. I'll freshen up myself."

"I don't like the thought of leaving you alone."

"I'll be fine. I'll lock the door and keep my cell phone close."

"Okay." He jogged toward the front room, grabbing his phone and keys. "You're sure?"

"I'm fine. Go."

He stepped close enough for me to detect the heat from his body. My stomach fluttered. His lips planted a kiss on my forehead. He paused, looking me in the eyes then sprinted out the front door.

I let out the breath I held. Chase Carson, you have no idea what you're doing to me!

He returned within the thirty minutes he had promised, and we finally made our way into the study.

"I haven't finished going through the desk yet. I think we should start there."

I sat down in the desk chair and started with the drawer where I had located the ledger. Further down I found a small accordion file. Inside were invoices from a Megan Foster. "Mmm. This looks interesting. Invoices for some kind of service." I continued my study of the page. "This indicates payment for disks."

"Hey, maybe that's her typist." Chase rose from his place on the couch and crossed to me. He stood behind me looking over my shoulder to study the paper with me.

I twisted around in my chair. "Oh, yeah, you did say she had a typist."

"Yes, she told me she wrote everything out and then sent it away to be typed. She had it put on a CD so that we could take that back to publish the book."

His face was so near to mine, I could smell remnants of maple syrup as he spoke and the clean aroma of shampoo. I snapped back to the topic at hand, turning back to the document I held.

"I wonder if there is any contact information. Do you think the typist kept copies?"

"I'm not sure about the arrangement they had. Could be possible that she saved it on her computer."

I sat up straight. "But, wait, you said you knew the book was complete. Do you know for sure if she had received it from this typist?" I waved the paper.

"No, I guess I assumed when she said it was complete that she meant she had the CD already. I really never thought about the fact that she might have meant her part was done. There is a chance." Chase's tone sounded hopeful.

We began to scan through the other documents until we found the contact information. "She lives in the next county over."

"Let's pay her a visit, shall we?" Chase tilted his head, gazing into my eyes expectantly.

"Okay."

I shoved the address into my purse. We jumped into Chase's rental car like we were two bloodhounds in hot pursuit.

We located Ms. Foster's house an hour later. We stepped to the front stoop and rang the doorbell. A young woman opened the door.

"Ms. Megan Foster?" I said.

"Yes?" Her brows rose.

"Hi, my name is Alex Lyndon. You typed for my grandmother, Olivia Lyndon. Oh, but you probably knew her as Alexa Livingston."

Ms. Foster's eyes grew wide and she looked suddenly afraid. "I don't know any information about her. She sends a manuscript, and I type it." She held her hands up as if surrendering.

"Ma'am, don't misunderstand. We aren't here to get information about her. I realize she was very confidential." I lowered my voice and looked into her eyes. "I'm not sure you have heard, but my grandmother passed away."

She pushed the door open wider and motioned us inside. "Please, sit."

"Thank you." I took a seat on the couch, and Chase slid in beside me.

"You say you are Miss Livingston's granddaughter?"

"Yes, ma'am. We are looking for her last manuscript. We thought you still might have it." I leaned forward, expectant and hopeful.

She shook her head. "Oh, no, I sent that to her. I know she received it because she called to thank me. She is, or was, such a nice woman. I'm sorry to hear she passed. I have always enjoyed doing her work." She grinned sheepishly. "I'm a fan of her books, so I always got to read it first before the public. Perk of the job, I guess." She shrugged.

"Would you by chance have a copy of the manuscript on your computer?" I asked, hopeful.

Ms. Foster shook her head. "No. Miss Olivia asked me to please not save any copies of her work on my computer after typing it."

"Strange."

"Oh, don't get me wrong. She was never rude about it. That was just her way. I respected her so I honored her wishes." Ms. Foster pursed her lips then continued. "Miss Olivia was particular. She had me put the manuscript on a CD."

Chase chuckled. "Yeah, I tried to get her to let me help her buy a newer laptop, but she said that her old desktop sufficed for what she needed. She had learned to put the CD in and look at the typed version. I usually converted it immediately to a flash drive." He stroked his chin and grinned. "I guess I felt the same as Ms. Foster. I just honored her ways. I figured, she was ninety." He shrugged.

"I'm sorry if we bothered you." My tone was loaded with disappointment.

"I'm sorry for your loss, for all our loss."

"You seemed rather skittish when we mentioned Miss Livingston," Chase said.

"Yes, I'm sorry about that. I prided myself on keeping Miss Olivia's secret. I knew I was among a very few who knew who Alexa Livingston really was."

We left Meagan Foster's house exactly in the same position as before—baffled as to the whereabouts of that manuscript. On the drive back to the house, we kept going over and over what we knew about the manuscript, trying to sort through any clues we might have overlooked. I was weary.

As we rounded the corner and the house came into sight, I gasped. "The front door is open!"

Chase slowed the car and stopped at the curb. "Would anyone have access to the house other than you?"

"Not that I know of." I started to get out, but Chase's arm restrained me.

"No, I'm calling the police. I would rather be wrong and have to apologize to someone."

Within a few moments a police car arrived with two officers.

Chase looked me directly in the eyes. "Stay here."

He jumped out of the car and approached the officers, gesturing toward the house. As the policemen entered the front door, each of them had a hand on his gun. I shivered. In a few minutes they emerged with Brant Collins. His hands were handcuffed behind his back. I jumped from the car. "Brant! What are you doing here in my house?"

Brant's head hung low until I finished my question. He then looked at me with sorrowful eyes. "I'm sorry, Miss Lyndon. I respected Miss Olivia better than to do this."

"Who are you?" Chase said.

Brant looked at him and then back at me. "I was telling the truth. I am just a resident here, and I have been caring for your grandmother's grounds. But, not long ago, a man approached me with a lucrative offer. He said if I could find a manuscript that your grandmother had written, he would make it worth my while. I'm sorry."

Chase questioned him further as I ran to the house to see if Brant had done any damage.

Chase met me at the entry. "It was a rival publisher. I know them."

"But, how could that be? I mean, wasn't Granny under contract with your company?"

"Well, yes and no. Miss Olivia was particular about each book she wrote. She insisted on contracting each one after completing it and showing it to me. That's another reason I came personally to retrieve her manuscripts. I brought the contract along for her sign. I always knew we would accept them, but she wasn't pretentious."

"Whoa. So this other company could have tricked me into signing that contract?"

He nodded and glanced around. "Is everything okay? He didn't mess up anything, did he?"

"No, thank goodness." I crossed my arms over my chest.

"He admitted to being your midnight intruder as well."

I crossed to Granny's favorite chair and plopped into it. I took a deep breath and let it out of puffed cheeks slowly.

Chase sat down across from me, leaned forward and looked into my eyes again as he had several times today. "Look, this has been stressful. Let's get our minds off this. Let me take you to dinner."

"Are you asking me on a date?" I conjured up my best teasing yet flirty expression.

He grinned. "Do you want it to be?"

"I asked you first." I tilted my head.

He stroked his chin. "I'll pick you up at six."

"Okay."

He walked slowly to the front door and glanced back at me every few steps. He paused when he opened the door and smiled at me before he slipped out.

I let out the breath I had been holding. He was so attractive in every way, but I wasn't sure what he saw in me. Suddenly my stomach filled with fluttering butterflies. "What will I wear?"

I jumped up and headed for the bedroom. I flung open the closet doors and stared as if something might leap out at me. Finally I started to pull out tops and bottoms and dresses. Some were automatically a no, so I tossed them onto the bed. After about twenty minutes, the reject pile was quite high. I settled on a simple dress. I stared at my reflection in the mirror, hoping for some inspiration on what to do with my hair and makeup. With only about half an hour before Chase would arrive, I decided to use a clip to put my hair up. Maybe that would make me look more sophisticated.

CHAPTER EIGHT

How LONG HAD it been since Chase Carson had been on a date? A real date. One he truly wanted to go on? He wasn't sure he had been on any such date until the promise of his date with Alex. He thanked God for giving him the courage to ask her. His strong feelings for her had developed in such a short period of time. Could love occur that quickly, or was this just infatuation? He so enjoyed her company. A sudden need to protect Alex at all costs rose in him. Was she feeling some of these same feelings toward him? If she did, what could their next date be, and where could they go? Chase shook his head. Reality hit him like a punch in the stomach. The manuscript. It was crucial to find it and take it immediately back to New York. The publishing company worked on a schedule with release dates held firmly. He wanted to locate the book so production could happen, but then again, he dreaded finding it. When that book was found, he would have to rush it back. That meant leaving Alex. He felt like a conflicted character from one of Miss Olivia's books.

He scrolled down to his mother's phone number and hit the button. She answered on the first ring. "Hey! How are things? How's Alex?"

He let out a snicker. "Alex is fine. We're going out tonight. She has had a lot going on, and I want to take her out to help her forget about it for a bit."

"Sounds good."

"I hope it will help relieve some stress." He sighed.

"What is it? I heard something in your voice just then."

He chuckled. "You know me too well, Mom."

"That's what Mamas do."

"I just, well, I know we need to find that manuscript, but…"

"But, that means you have to leave there to bring it home," his mother finished.

"Exactly. I sound crazy, don't I?" He plopped onto the side of the bed.

"Nope, not crazy, maybe in love."

He tried to laugh that comment off, but to him his attempt sounded fake. "Mom, I just met her. How could I be in love?"

"I don't know. Ask the Good Lord. I can hear it in your voice."

"What do you hear?"

"Something I've never heard there before. Don't fight it, Chase. Maybe this is God ordained."

"You really think so?" He recalled the feel of Alex in his arms and craved more of her nearness.

"Have you been praying about God's direction for your life?"

"Yeah." He shrugged.

"Well, then, there you go."

Could his mother be right? Had God set all this in motion? Or, was this just wishful thinking and trying to force something that wasn't there?

After talking a few more moments with his mother, they signed off. He called his assistant in New York to give an update.

"Chase, hey, good to hear from you. So, how's it going? Do you have the manuscript?"

"Not exactly." Chase doodled on the hotel notepad.

"What does that mean?"

"The author didn't leave us word on where to find the book. We have to hunt for it.'

"We?"

"Yes, the author's granddaughter and I. As soon as we have it, I'll get back to you. I know we're working on a deadline. I just had no idea about her death and all."

"I'll let them know here about this update." Carol paused. "So, this granddaughter ..." Curiosity dripped from her tone. She had known Chase for several years. In fact, she had been with the company long enough that she was more like family than an employee.

Chase tried to keep his voice nonchalant and matter of fact. "Her name is Alex. Can you believe she didn't even know her grandmother was an author until I told her?"

"Really? Is Alex your age?"

Chase could see where Carol was headed with her question. "Yes. Thanks for relaying the update. As soon as I find the manuscript, I'll rush it back."

"No hurry." She giggled. "Oh, Chase?"

"Yeah?"

"Wear a blue or teal shirt with that blazer with the elbow patches."

Chase rolled his eyes. "Thanks for the tip."

Chase once again inhaled and let out a heavy sigh. He proceeded to pray that God would help them to locate that manuscript. But, he also prayed that God might show him what to do about Alex. Just her name warmed him and sent his heart reeling. Maybe he would take Carol's advice on his outfit. He laughed at himself and shook his head. When had Chase Carson ever been so concerned with his wardrobe?

CHAPTER NINE

AT ONLY MINUTES before six, I surveyed the end product in Granny's antique standup mirror. I shrugged at my reflection. "Still just plain ol'Alex." I could almost hear Granny Olivia scold me for saying that.

Out of the corner of my eye I saw a car pull up outside. I inhaled, puffing out my cheeks and exhaled through pursed lips. I skipped down the steps just in time for the knock. Upon opening the door, words stuck in my throat. Chase's sandy-brown hair was tamed behind his ears. I was sure Granny Olivia must have encouraged him to get a haircut often, but I found it rather attractive. He had a casual blazer on that was almost the color of his hair, a pale teal shirt which brought out the hue of his eyes, and dark jeans. He pulled his arm from behind his back and produced a small bouquet of roses. All I could do at first was gasp.

Finally, I managed to speak. "Thank you. They're beautiful." I took the flowers from him. "Let me put these in some water."

He followed me into the kitchen and leaned against the countertop. "You look lovely."

Instantly heat crept onto my face and down my neck. "Thank you. You're looking mighty handsome yourself." I busied my attention with the bouquet so my face could cool. Then, I stepped back. "There, I think I'll put these in the other room where they'll be seen more."

Once again he trailed me like a heeling puppy. After placing the bouquet on the living room table, I turned to face him. "That's perfect."

"Yes, you are quite perfect." He grinned.

"No, I meant…"

"I said what I meant." He winked.

There went the heat to my face again. My heart was doing flip-flops and somersaults.

"Shall we?" He gave a slight bow toward the front door.

"Yes."

Chase impressed me with his chivalrous ways. He opened the car door for me to get in and then back out when we arrived at the restaurant. He offered his arm, and I placed my hand through it. Finally we made our way to our table and sat down across from one another.

"You seem to know all about me. What about you? Who is Chase Carson?" I leaned forward, resting my elbows on the table.

"Well, the publishing company was actually my father's. I wasn't sure what I wanted to do, so in the meantime, I worked at the company editing." He took a sip of water. "That's how I met your grandmother. I started editing her books. At the time, I could travel to Tennessee, work with her, and then take back the finished product. About two years ago my father died suddenly of a massive heart attack, so there I was—I was in charge. At first I wasn't sure I wanted the responsibility, but I found I truly like putting out books of worth, with a Christian message. I had stopped my editing, giving it over to others, but I just couldn't do that with Miss Olivia. I continued to come here, edit her work, which needed very little editing, and then deliver it back personally. I had become much too attached to Miss Olivia not to come for her manuscripts myself."

I smiled. "I hope she rubbed off on me. I mean, she made a difference, you know? Me? I don't think so." I diverted my eyes to my diet soda, stirring it with my straw.

Chase grabbed one of my hands and held it gently. "We're not all called to the same thing. You have your place in God's plan."

"How do you know? Up until now I feel like I've accomplished nothing. I have wasted thirty years just spinning my wheels. Always planning to start my life. Granny obviously took advantage of all opportunities for the Lord, so He used her to touch many. I've done nothing." I bowed my head. I couldn't look Chase in the eyes after admitting that to him. I was ashamed. His fingertips lifted my chin and tingles traveled up my jaw.

"It's never too late with God to find the life He has for you. I think He's working that plan even now." His eyes seemed to look all the way to my heart.

My pulse picked up a notch. I was glad our food came at that moment, because I was at a loss for words.

After praying for our meal, Chase chuckled.

"What?"

"I was just remembering the first time I was sent to meet Miss Olivia. I thought my father was setting me up. Then Miss Olivia opened that door wearing—"

"Her Hawaiian shirt," I finished. We both laughed.

By the time dinner was through, I had bared my soul with him about my broken marriage and various jobs. Granny had shared much of my trials with Chase already.

He leveled his gaze at me. "You know, she was proud of you."

"I'm not sure what she had to be proud of." I bit my bottom lip, warding off a quiver of sadness and regret.

"She always bragged about you and showed me recent pictures of you. I think she was trying to do a little matchmaking." Chase winked at me with a wide grin on his face.

I rolled my eyes and shook my head at the thought. "I know she told me she was proud of me, but I guess I thought that was just the grandmother in her. That's what they're supposed to do."

"She was proud of your character and rightfully so. You held onto your faith through it all. That's strength."

I was undeserving of any compliments on my character or faith. "I suppose I feel I've been made for more." My eyes suddenly misted over.

"I think you have. You just have to discover it."

I swallowed and nodded. Was Chase right? Was there a purpose God would entrust to me, not for fame, but, like Granny, for his glory? What other goal was worthy anyway? Even though I found a true monetary inheritance in Granny's Word, she would still say the greatest inheritance was the words from the Bible itself. My eyes suddenly widened, and my mouth flew open.

"What? What is it?" Chase's tone evidenced concern.

"I think I know where the manuscript is. Let's go!" I took Chase's hand and practically dragged him to the car. I fidgeted in the passenger's seat. It seemed to take extra-long to get back to the house. Finally we pulled into the driveway, and I rushed through the front door. Chase followed without a word. I approached the coffee table in the living room. There it was. The big family Bible. "Wait right here."

I rushed to retrieve the will letter Granny had written. Sure enough as I reread it there was the clue. *My final words* and *your inheritance*. The money was only one of the things Granny had left to me. The other was also hidden in the Word. I knelt before the heirloom Bible and slowly opened the cover. There was an envelope with my name on it and a computer disk. "Right in front of my eyes the whole time."

I held the disk up to Chase. He smiled and took it. I sat down in the favorite chair and began to read.

Dear Alex (and Chase)…

I looked up at Chase and smiled, showing him his name on the letter.

Finding the inheritance means you know my secret. I hope you don't think me devious. I had to support my little family in some way. Many in my situation have to resort to procuring employment at Wal-Mart and such. God blessed me beyond belief when I could actually make money by spinning my tales in writing. I told the Lord it was never about fame so that is why the pen name. He gave me the ideas and the imagination, and I wrote it down. After hearing the effects of that first book, salvations and rededications, I was "hooked" as one might say. The very thought that my imagination-born stories could encourage another in their walk with the Lord pushed me to continue all these years. With this letter is the last in the series. The end of the story, if you will. My life's story has come to an end and now I get to bask in the glory. Not mine, but His. I do hope I might meet some of the people I encouraged when they get here—my inheritance, laid up in heaven where nothing can ever touch it. I draw from a quote I once saw on a plaque, "Life is God's novel, but you must let Him write it." My precious Alex, let Him write the story of your life. It will be a beautiful one.
I love you,
Granny Olivia (aka Alexa Livingston)

I sat with tears streaming down my cheeks. Chase's cheeks were wet as well. He crossed to me and lifted me to my feet. He wrapped his arms around me, and I returned the embrace. We clung to each other for several moments. The emotions within me were varied. I grieved the loss of Granny. I cried from a hope deep inside. I cried from gratefulness to God. As we pulled away from one another, Chase placed his hands gently on the sides of my face, holding my head in his hands. A tingling sensation rushed down my body. I trembled at his intimate touch. His breath was warm against my cheek as he moved closer and kissed my lips ever so slightly. We were awakened from the dreamy moment by the ringing of the phone. Reluctantly, I moved away from Chase to answer it, leaving him in the living room alone.

"Honey, this is Millie. Is everything okay? Have you found what you were looking for?"

"Oh, yes." I did think I'd found what I was looking for.

"What, dear?"

"Sorry, Millie, we were able to find what we had been searching for. Thank you." I didn't want to be rude to Millie, but I wanted to return to the living room to see if I was right. Had I found what I was looking for? Not the manuscript…but more.

I hurried back toward the living room. "Sorry, that was Millie…" I froze when I saw Chase holding a journal in his hands.

He held the book up, shaking it in my direction. His eyes were wide. "Is this another of your grandmother's stories? It's really good. I think we could work with this." He glanced around the room. "She probably has a lot of these around that we could go through. Maybe her story isn't complete after all."

In his excitement, I couldn't bring myself to tell him that the journal was mine. I wasn't sure why.

"What a day! It's getting late. I better get back to the hotel so we both can crash. See you tomorrow morning?"

I nodded, and he kissed me lightly on the mouth again. After seeing him out, I leaned against the front door, thinking about this day. Granny had written that life is God's novel. Was God writing Chase into the story of my life? I meandered toward the bedroom. The only problem with that plotline was that I was a small-town girl who would never fit into a bustling New York City. Chase was probably used to that lifestyle. Granny's house stood near the picturesque mountains and had proven to be home for me. Living here was part of God's plan for my life.

Chase now had what he had been looking for—the manuscript. He needed to fly back and get it published. He would forget about me. He didn't have time in his busy schedule for someone so messed up. My heart ached at the thought. Why had I let myself fall for a guy I couldn't have? When would I get that beautiful story Granny spoke of in her letter?

I slid between the covers of the four-poster bed. My emotions pushed my pen through my journal at a rapid speed. By the time I closed my eyes to sleep it was two in the morning. I had to write, for it was as if God whispered an outline into my ear, and I had to put it down before it blew away. Just before falling asleep I realized the outline was the story of Granny Olivia's life. It had to be written. Her readers needed to know who Alexa Livingston really was. They needed to know she loved them even though she never laid eyes on their precious faces. Well, the readers might never read this story, but I had to write it.

CHAPTER TEN

CHASE HATED TO leave Alex, but he feared his emotions would get the best of him. He needed to think without the distraction of her precious face. He had no choice. He had to return to New York with the manuscript. Even now his heart was still back at Miss Olivia's house with Alex. However, did Alex feel the same about him? They had met mere days ago. Her feelings might not match his. He contemplated his feelings for her. It felt like love, but would he recognize that should it happen? Maybe this was a simple fascination. Still the fact loomed. He had to return to New York. He had responsibilities. He settled on intense prayer about his feelings while away from Alex. Possibly a conversation with his mom could help sort his feelings. That would be his game plan, even though leaving Alex would prove painful.

He popped the manuscript disk into his laptop and began reading. He shook his head and sighed. *Miss Olivia could sure make words dance.*

After reading the first chapter, there were no editor's marks to be made. What a loss to the writing world. He recalled the journal he had found back at the house. He would encourage Alex to set aside any other story remnants she might find as she went through

Miss Olivia's things. There was a chance this manuscript didn't have to be the last story Alexa Livingston told.

MY SLUMBER ENDED with a knock echoing up the stairs. I rolled over and moaned. Suddenly I realized the sun was up and the knocking must have been Chase. I leapt from the bed and sprinted down the stairs. I squinted upon opening the door. When my eyes began to adjust, Chase was looking me over and grinning, eyebrows raised.

"Did I wake you?" His voice was full of sarcasm.

I looked down at my crumpled pajamas and back to him. "Nope, it's a new look," I shot back with an equal amount of sarcasm.

We both broke forth in laughter.

I stepped to the side and motioned. "Come in. I'm sorry. I know I look like a total train wreck."

"If a train wreck can be adorable, then I agree."

My ears blazed hot. I propped my hand on my hip. "Adorable, please. This? You can't be serious. Maybe you need your eyes checked."

"Nope." His expression softened, and I was swept into his arms. He kissed me and then stepped back. "My eyesight is fine."

I was having trouble catching my breath.

"But, seriously, did you have trouble sleeping? I crashed."

"I guess…a little trouble."

His brow knitted. "Why?"

"Well, I had to do something before I could fall asleep."

"Did you look through more of your granny's things?" Chase shoved his hands into his jeans pockets and glanced around.

"No. I had to write something."

"Oh?"

"Do you believe in epiphanies? You know, like God telling you something that you have to write down?"

He tilted his head. "I suppose. Remember, I'm not a writer. I just edit."

"Well, God just wouldn't let me go to sleep until I had written down an outline."

"An outline?" His brow crinkled.

"Yeah. An outline for a story about Granny Olivia's life."

"Maybe this writing thing is in the genes, huh?" He adjusted my pajama collar. His lack of sincerity flustered me. "Oh, by the way, if you find any more of those journals your granny left behind, let me know. The one I picked up last night probably has other parts that go with it because it was more like the middle of the story."

I nodded. I still couldn't bring myself to tell him the journal he had read from last evening was mine.

"Now you need to get dressed. I'm taking you to breakfast. My plane leaves for New York at noon."

His tone evidenced an excitement to return to New York. But, New York was his home. He was probably glad to be returning there.

"You sit. I'll hurry."

"I'm good. I have some calls to make and some texts and emails to send." He pulled out his phone, meandered to the couch, and plopped down. "Need to let everyone know I'm coming back with the manuscript."

When he mentioned the manuscript his face lit up. He had accomplished his mission. In a way, I wished we hadn't found the disk so soon. Now I only had until noon before Chase would leave me for his real life. My demeanor was sure to show the sadness I was feeling.

The ride to the restaurant was quiet. As we sat across from each other at the diner, the silence hung heavy.

"Hey, you seem down or distracted. What's wrong?" Chase's head tilted to one side, and his eyes probed mine.

I shrugged. "I don't know." I picked at the food on my plate with my fork.

Chase lifted my chin with his fingertips. "Come back with me to New York."

My jaw dropped. I never expected him to ask me that. My mind was fuzzy for a moment. I shook my head. "I would never fit in there."

"How would you know? You've never been there with me." His eyes widened, and his face took on an expectant expression.

A heaviness spread through my chest. "But you have a life there and work."

Chase glanced at his watch. "I wish I had more time, but I do have to get back with this book of your granny's. Can I call you?"

"Of course."

I fought a painful lump in my throat that threatened to burst forth as tears. I barely heard what Chase was chattering on about. He was excited about finding the book before it was found by someone else or stolen. I was glad we had found it as well. Granny's last book deserved to be printed. I truly was happy to know her readers would have the end of the story. My feelings had no connection to any of that. I had allowed myself to enjoy Chase's company way too much. I hadn't thought ahead when I had allowed myself to fall for him. Now I was paying for the fact that he must leave. This was inevitable. I had blocked out that thought until now.

Chase walked me to the door. He appeared sad to go. He kissed me, lingering on my lips. Finally, he glanced at his watch again and sighed. "I've got to go or I'll miss my flight. I'll be in touch." He sprinted down the walk and jumped into his rental car. He waved and I returned his wave with a feeble one of my own.

His car disappeared down the street. I moved in slow motion into the house. The silence was deafening. I plopped into my favorite chair in the living room. I wouldn't hear from Chase personally again. Just his signature on the royalty checks. It was fun while it lasted.

THE MORE MILES between he and Alex, the heavier Chase's heart became. Certainly, he was glad to find the manuscript, but that excitement was dampened because he had to leave her. Finally back in his own apartment, he struggled for at least some degree of comfort. His home had never felt so empty, nor had the New York noise seemed so accentuated. He closed his eyes imagining what Alex might be doing right now. Her face wasn't difficult to conjure in his mind's eye. He could picture her sitting in that chair in the living room or even standing at the kitchen counter making pancakes.

Had she thought of him since his departure? Would she consider coming to New York to visit? She might enjoy being here for the debut of Miss Olivia's book. Surely he could convince her to come for that, even if she didn't want to come for him. He hoped some part of her might come just to see him. Whatever it took, Chase had to see Alex again. In fact, he craved the sound of her voice before he could think of trying to go to sleep tonight. He pulled out his cell phone and scrolled down to her number. His finger hovered above the button. Was he being too pushy? He definitely didn't want to push her away or seem too eager. Finally, he pushed the send button with as much courage as he could muster.

CHAPTER ELEVEN

I MOSEYED INTO the study and reached into the closet to retrieve another journal.

Granny, I'm not sure I can do your story justice, but I feel I'm supposed to try. Actually, I have to write it. It won't leave me alone.

I sat down at Granny's writing desk. Words began to flow. My hand could hardly keep up. The next time I chanced to look at the clock across the room, evening had come. I put my pencil down and stretched. I carried my journal and pencil into the kitchen where I popped some popcorn and grabbed a diet soda. I juggled it all up the stairs to the bedroom. I changed into my pajamas and propped myself in the bed. I alternated between crunching on my snack and continuing my writing. My cell phone buzzed, breaking the silence, and I jumped.

"Hello?"

"What are you doing?"

It was Chase. My breath caught momentarily in my throat. He had called! I wanted to do a little happy dance, but I calmed myself. "I'm eating popcorn in bed."

"Do you have on those adorable pajamas you had on the other day?"

I giggled. "I wouldn't call them adorable, comfortable maybe, but not adorable."

"Matter of opinion."

"Are you home?"

"Yeah, but I miss you, Alex. Will you at least come to New York for the debut of your granny's book?" His voice held a bit of a whine.

I bit my bottom lip. "Maybe."

"Maybe?"

"I'm not sure I would fit in there. I guess I see why Granny Olivia stayed incognito. I do better that way too."

"Please come for me." There was a long silence and then he spoke again. "Think about it, okay? I'll be in touch."

"Okay. Thank you for calling."

"You're welcome. And, Alex, I...Goodnight."

"Goodnight."

As I put my phone on the bedside table, I was still in shock Chase had called. He said he missed me. But, did he just miss me casually as a friend? I missed him. More than casually. Could we have begun a serious relationship in the short amount of time he was here? Was I slipping into my hopeless romantic act? After the mess that was my first marriage, I wasn't sure how to do this thing called love. Did I even know what love was? I wanted to know and experience it, but it might be too late for me.

My journal beckoned again, and I continued to write Granny's story. My hand began to ache, and I reluctantly stopped for the night. As I placed my journal and pencil on the bedside table, the framed picture of Granny and me caught my eye.

"Granny, is this how the writing came to you?"

I wished she were here. I had so many questions I would ask her, knowing what I knew now. Wait, why not take a trip to the bookstore? Why hadn't I thought of that before? I needed to read Granny's books. I was so anxious to find and read her books I could barely go to sleep.

The next morning I sprang from the bed. I showered and dressed and headed to a little bookstore I had seen on the other side of town. I purchased every book the store had that had been penned by Granny.

The beautiful fall day compelled me to sit on the screened-in porch. I opened the cover of the first book and dove in. By the second sentence I found myself transported into the world of the story. With each page I turned I found goose bumps on my arms or misty eyes or sometimes even a chuckle. No wonder she was a bestselling author.

When I took a break to make a sandwich, I grabbed some loose leaf paper. I needed to take some notes on the writing techniques I noticed in Granny's book. Late that evening I finished the first book. I had scrawled several pages of notes. I stared at the book's cover. Where might I find Granny's rough drafts? She was inclined to write in longhand and then have someone else type. One place I hadn't explored yet was the attic.

I rushed to the small hall between the bedroom and bathroom. A short string hung from the ceiling. I stood on tiptoes and pulled it. A panel lowered, and a ladder glided down to the floor in front of me. I mounted the first rung and prayed I wouldn't encounter any bats. My mother had had trouble with those gruesome flying rodents in her crawlspace and had to call an exterminator. I climbed slowly. Another string hung down as I neared the top. Upon pulling it, light flooded the attic. I waited a moment, holding my breath. Nothing. I sighed with relief. A musty smell accosted my nostrils.

When my head popped up above the attic floor level, several plastic totes came into view. I hoisted myself the rest of the way up. The totes weren't labeled. I would just have to open them. I approached the nearest one and snapped off the lid. Jackpot! The tote was filled with green journals. I picked one up and opened the cover. On the front page was printed in Granny's handwriting— *Until We Meet Again—Chapter Three.*

I remembered that book. I had purchased that one at the bookstore. If this was here, I was sure I could find the book I finished reading today. I started to snap off lids and check for the title. The fifth crate brought success. I searched until I located the journals for the first few chapters. I climbed back down the ladder with my find and replaced the attic door. I rushed to the bedroom and spread out the journals, my notes, and the finished novel. I studied the journals comparing them with the completed novel. This was like being in a private writing class with Granny as the teacher. If I couldn't talk to her personally about writing and strategies, this was the next best thing,

I must have given in to exhaustion at some point, because I woke up lying across the bed with journals around me and on my chest. I stumbled to the kitchen for some sustenance. I could hardly wait to finish eating. I had a new story idea of my own buzzing in my head I needed to write down. I prayed God would allow the stories He was giving to hold meaning for someone. I had no hopes of being as good as Alexa Livingston, but I was beginning to understand the allure of writing Granny had possessed.

Chase had called every other night since he had left. Three weeks had passed. I hadn't told him what I had been doing when he called. I laughed, imagining what people must think of me. I had concentrated on writing so much, I had been a recluse for these past weeks. I had at least started attending church—Granny's church. I immediately could see why she enjoyed being there. It was a warm place. The pastor preached the Word. I would never forget the day I walked forward in the church to make the best and biggest decision of my life.

I sat down Sunday morning in the seat I remembered was Granny's. The opening hymn twanged out in familiar southern drawl. During the fellowship song several people greeted me with hugs and smiles. I sensed God's presence with us in that small sanctuary. I had a sudden realization that this place and these people were all a part of who Granny was as well. After the service I noticed a Circle meeting scheduled for the next morning at ten listed on the announcement section of the bulletin.

"Millie, was this Granny's Circle group?" I pointed to the printed announcement.

"Yes, the same one I'm in."

"Do you think the other women would mind if I came and sat in?"

"No, child. I'm sure they'd love it." She patted my shoulder.

Was Millie right about the ladies not minding if I visited to their meeting? The more I learned about Granny, the more I realized that I truly didn't know her. I wanted to know her more, and this was the best way. She would have liked knowing I was involved in the church and the things of God.

When I entered the church's small fellowship hall, there was already a group of women sitting around a long rectangular table. There were probably ten of them, all white or gray-haired. I definitely brought the age in the room way down by my presence. Millie waved me over to a chair near her. I must have been the last one expected, because a lady at the end of the table began immediately when I sat down.

"We are glad to have Alex Lyndon with us today." She smiled my way, and I returned her welcome with a smile and a nod.

She proceeded to have their program, which was from their mission magazine. Millie elbowed me lightly to indicate I could share hers. After that, they went right into discussing what type of projects they wanted to be involved with this month. Before I knew it, they were sharing Granny's love for different service projects as well as her continued involvement throughout her time as a member of their group.

"I'm sure they are missing Miss Olivia down at the shelter and soup kitchen. She never missed her shifts at either one," a petite woman said.

"Yes, we should try to make sure her times are covered. We could never live up to her devotion, but we could certainly offer to give assistance nonetheless."

"You're right. She did love her work there. I do wish she could have realized her dream to go on a mission trip."

"Well, now I think she went on one anytime she helped anywhere she found herself."

"She did get to send Alex's mother. That was the next best thing from what she said."

All of the women nodded in unison. I had to bite my lip to keep from giggling. When the meeting was over they invited me for their luncheon. I started to decline, but they were persistent. During lunch, many of the ladies told me about specific projects Granny headed. She had made a difference in her community as well as her church and friends. It was obvious she didn't talk about her faith, she lived it out. This was yet another part of the story of Granny's life that had to be included. I was tired from just considering the schedule Granny kept. How did she get everything done? What an amazing woman! With all her accomplishments, how could she ever have been proud of me? I was suddenly humbled and challenged all at once.

CHAPTER TWELVE

CHASE WAS ABOUT three-fourths of the way through Miss Olivia's manuscript, *Haply Ever After*. He was excited and saddened all at the same time. This novel had to be the best, most appropriate for the last installment. However, to think that this writing talent was gone was hard to swallow. Alex came to mind, and he immediately pulled out his cell phone to call her.

"Hey, how are things?" Her upbeat tone quickened his pulse.

"Good. This latest novel of Miss Olivia's is outstanding." He propped his forearms on the desk.

"It would have to be. I've had the opportunity to read more of her earlier works. What can I say? She was awesome."

"Yeah, I just hate that this is it. By the way, did you find any more journals or manuscripts?"

"Umm, no, but I'll let you know if I do." Suddenly her tone sounded awkward after his inquiry.

"Is everything okay?"

"Sure, I'll keep looking."

"Okay. The debut is getting closer. Are you going to take me up on my offer and come?"

"I don't know. I'd like to, but..."

"Don't turn me down." He paused and cleared his throat. "Just keep thinking about it. I want it to be a tribute to Miss Olivia."

"I'm sure it will be great."

After saying goodbyes, Chase sat still, staring. Alex's strange reaction to his question about the journals still bothered him. Maybe it was just his imagination.

"Mr. Carson, could I come in? We need to talk," his assistant said.

"Sure, come on in. Your expression and tone tells me I'm not going to like what you're about to say."

"You're right. You're not going to like it." Before she sat down in the chair on the other side of the desk, she laid a stack of various sized and colored papers in front of him.

He glanced at the headline of the newspaper article on top— "Author Comes Out of the Closet in New Book Series." He looked up into Carol's eyes.

She nodded. "It's Stephanie Rader."

Chase leaned back in his chair and ran his hand through his hair. "So, give me the low down."

"She is debuting a new secular series. Reports and reviews say the content is quite racy to say the least. We'll have to make a statement about where we stand, and what we will do with her books."

Chase closed his eyes, willing this nightmare to go away. The company stood for godly morals and values. If these new books contained questionable content, then their reaction should be to remove the books they had published with this author. They would need to issue a statement about why they would do so. Chase opened his eyes.

"I know what we have to do, but we're going to take some hits, not only from the media, but from our pockets."

"I know. First, why don't you let me get the author in here to talk? She has violated part of the contract she has with us. There is a morality clause."

Chase nodded. "Okay, let me know how soon she can come in."

"I will." Carol stood and started toward the door but turned back. "Hey, it's okay. God wasn't caught off guard."

"You're right. That's exactly what Dad would have said." He grinned.

"I know. That's why I said it. I heard him say it several times." She smiled at Chase as she closed his office door behind her.

Chase sat in the silence of his office. What would his father do right now if he were here? As soon as the answer came, he found himself kneeling in prayer on the floor beside his desk.

CHAPTER THIRTEEN

AFTER TALKING WITH Chase, I decided to do exactly as I said I would. I searched for other journals. I didn't have to go far. I was seated in the living room chair that had become as popular a spot with me as it had been with Granny. I had never noticed the side table near the chair had a magazine rack underneath. Three journals stared back at me. I grabbed them and began thumbing through. My eyes bugged when I realized these were personal journals, not story journals. The last entry was dated just days before she died.

My time in this world is nearing an end, but I have no fear. God has given me a full life, a rewarding life I never deserved. I look forward to being greeted by my sweet daughter. The thought that finally Hayward had the opportunity to meet his daughter is also a comfort. He has had some time with her himself now. It has been too many years since I have looked into the eyes of my beloved Hayward. I only regret that I never could prove his murder. I know it would never have brought him back, but I could have made sure greed didn't cause anyone else to suffer the loss I suffered. The only sorrow I feel for exiting this world is leaving my sweet Alex. I know God has plans for her beyond what she even knows.

Fresh tears trickled down my cheeks. It was truly amazing the faith Granny had in me, yet I didn't have in myself. Her words were so confident when she wrote that God had a plan for me. I wanted to believe it and realize it. What love she still held for her husband. What would it be like to have someone to love like Granny had? It was sad to think Granny was still haunted by her husband's death even days before her own death.

The information I had found about my grandfather's death still intrigued me. I sprinted up the steps to the bedroom and retrieved the shoebox containing the document about his death. I skimmed the newspaper article again. In 1950 there wasn't the same forensic technology we had access to now, however, the article suggested there was very little done to verify the cause of death. It seemed to be chalked up to accidental. But, Chase had mentioned a novel of Granny's that resembled this storyline. Since it was probably one of her first books, it might be difficult to secure a copy.

I carried the box downstairs with me and into the study. As I considered what archives might be available and even if there might be a remaining business partner to interview, I spotted a book on the shelf I hadn't noticed before. I drew closer to the shelf and gasped when I realized the book's title—*The Lone Survivor*. I immediately opened the cover and started to read. I read until my eyes burned. I finally finished the story the next afternoon. Chase was right. The plot was very close to what I had pieced together from the articles and written pages in the shoebox. Now I had to know if my grandfather had been murdered.

The best place to start would be Millie. I scurried across the yard and up to her door. Millie welcomed me in with a broad smile. She insisted on making me tea and served it in the teapot Granny had left to her.

"Millie, I'm wondering what you know about my grandfather's death. I found Granny's journal, and she was still bothered by his death, even right before she died."

"Well, I know there was no doubt in my mind either that his death was no accident." She shook her head.

"Really?"

"I was close enough to Olivia at that time to know that Hayward would hardly even take an aspirin, much less something stronger, which they said he overdosed on." She sipped her tea.

"There was something in the articles I found about his needing medication for some kind of accident he had?"

"Yes, poor man. He was into the actual building end of the business at first. During one of the jobs he fell from a roof and hurt his back. That's why I could be sure I also didn't believe the reports that he had strong pain medication. Olivia tried to get him to go to the doctor to get some kind of pain medicine, but he refused. He just didn't like taking pills."

"Hmmm. Why didn't someone listen when Granny reported that?"

"I'd say because the person that would have been guilty had connections with the law." She looked me directly in the eyes.

"What do you mean?"

"Your grandfather's partner, Mr. Cook, had himself connected and covered in many areas. He had done enough to help the community that people would turn the other way if he crossed the line, if you know what I mean." Millie's eyes narrowed.

"I see. Did you say Cook?" I pulled out a notepad from my purse.

"Yes—C-O-O-K."

"Have I seen that name around town?"

Millie nodded. "Yep, that's his son."

"Did Granny Olivia ever try to talk to him to see if he knew the story?"

"No, she stayed clear of the Cooks. She told me she had forgiven, but it was hard to forget. She joked it was easier to just stay away from them, so's not to lose her religion." She grinned.

I shook my head and chuckled.

After tea I sprinted back to the house to read through the shoebox information again. It seemed strange to me that a partner would kill another just because he wanted all of the income. Surely there was some other reason for such drastic measures as murder. I decided to pay a visit to the downtown Greeneville library. Maybe I could find more newspaper articles to piece this mystery together. I had discovered a journal entry in which Granny had admitted to stopping her newspaper subscription. She stated she was tired of the lies. She preferred not knowing what was being written about her husband and his partner.

I pulled into an empty spot in front of the library, and upon entering, I found a lady at the front desk. "Excuse me. Do you have past newspapers archived here? Several years back?"

"That would be at the other building up the street. The one on the corner with the large columns." The librarian gestured in the direction of the building.

"I know the one."

"We don't have the space here, so we send the archives there." The woman flashed a smile.

"Thank you."

I found a parking spot on the street and marched up to the columned building. The sign on the window indicated closing time to be five. I glanced at my watch—4:45. The papers would have to wait until tomorrow. There was no way I could even locate the periodicals in fifteen minutes, and I definitely couldn't examine them that quickly. I turned back toward my car and shuffled along. I hadn't quite made it into the driveway back at the house when Chase called.

CHAPTER FOURTEEN

STEPHANIE RADAR WAS due in Chase's office any moment. He had prayed continuously since being informed of the appointment. He needed to project his Christian values without jumping down the woman's throat. That was what the flesh side of him wanted to do.

His assistant's head popped through the door. "Mr. Carson, Ms. Radar is here." Carol nodded her support.

"Send her in."

Chase took a deep breath and exhaled slowly to try to release his tension.

"Mr. Carson," Ms. Radar said as she flourished into the room. She made herself at home by taking a seat in the chair across from Chase's desk. She simply ignored his outstretched hand.

Chase pulled his hand back in. "Ms. Radar." He seated himself again.

"I know what this is about." She sighed, picking lint off her skirt.

"I'm sure you do. You have put us in a position we don't like to be in."

"Look, I know this new release is different than what I've been writing for you, but there's no reason I can't do both." She shrugged.

Chase leaned forward, propping an arm on his desk. "Actually, there is a reason you can't do both. We have a contract with a morality clause. We feel strongly about the morals and values we portray in our books. That's why we have the clause."

Ms. Rader waved her hand dismissively. "Oh, come on Mr. Carson. You're gonna have to catch up. Most publishers now maintain an inspirational division in their company, but they publish other things, too. That's just keeping up with the times."

"We aren't trying to keep up with the times." He paused to lower his tone. "We are a Christian publishing company. Period. We can't continue to publish and distribute your books if you have others out there that go against what we promote. It sends a mixed message."

"Then, I suppose you'll have to do what you have to do. The secular company gave me a better advance anyway." She crossed her arms over her chest.

Chase's blood was on a slow simmer, yet he also had a wave of sadness. Stephanie Radar had sold out to making money. She came across so cold that he was rather taken aback. There would be extreme costs to Carson Publishing to pull her titles. This was the third author who had been sucked into the secular market.

"I'm sorry you feel that way. I can't hide my disappointment. My father established this company on Christian principles and made it his goal to produce books that would speak to readers' hearts for the sake of God. I still believe in that."

Ms. Rader shrugged. "Then, I guess we're done." She stood, spun on her heels, and left the office with a slam of his door.

It was only moments before Carol entered. "You okay?"

"Not really." He rolled his eyes. "I want to be angry, but I'm more saddened by the fact that these authors can just turn their backs on their Christian convictions so easily."

"I know. It's disturbing. This would have broken your father's heart." She patted her chest.

"Don't you know it. I wish he were here at times like this to help me."

"Chase, you know what he would do, even if it meant losing lots of money. He ran this place by his founding principles. That's why I'm still here." Carol straightened her shoulders.

"You're right." He gave an emphatic nod. "Pull the books."

"We'll have to give a statement." Carol scribbled notes onto her notepad.

"I know. Can we stall for a couple of days on that? I need to pray for the right words, you know?"

"Yes, I know. It will take a few days to get the books pulled. That should give you a little bit of time before a statement is required."

"Thanks." Chase tried to muster a smile for his faithful assistant.

"It'll be okay. You just keep doing right. You'll win in the end."

"Sounds like Proverbs."

"Yep, I was just reading that this morning. God's timing is perfect." She exited.

Suddenly Chase craved the sound of Alex's voice. He pulled out his phone and punched the button.

"Hey!" Her voice warmed him.

"Hello. What are you doing?"

"What's wrong, Chase? You sound down."

How had she learned so quickly to read him over the phone?

"I am down. Trouble with an author."

"Want to tell me about it? Might make you feel better."

Just hearing her voice boosted his doldrums, but he proceeded to tell her about Stephanie Radar.

"Wow, it amazes me what greed will make people do. I mean, it can make you turn your back on everything you've ever stood for. I won't say that could never happen to me because that would be arrogant, but I just wasn't raised that way."

"Me either. Enough of that. What have you been up to?" He leaned back in his chair.

"Well, I've turned into a regular Nancy Drew."

"What?"

"I found some of Granny's personal journals. It seems she was still haunted by the fact that her husband was murdered, but the perpetrators got away with it. I've been doing my own investigating."

"So, what have you found?" He rubbed at the tension in his neck.

"Not much more than we knew before, but hopefully a trip to the archives tomorrow will shed more light into this mystery."

"Now about the mystery of whether you are going to come to New York?"

"I might be talked into it, if you still want me there."

His heart skipped a beat. "If I still want you here? Yes, I want you here. I...miss you."

There was a long silence on the other end. "Alex?"

"Yeah?"

"I...I guess I'd better go. I'll be in touch. Don't doubt that I want you to come. I don't know how to convince you, but I'll find a way."

"That sounds mysterious." She giggled, and the sound warmed Chase to the core.

After saying goodbye, Chase propped his elbows on his desk. His mood was totally altered. Alex had lifted his spirits. His feelings for her ran deep, but could he tell her? The right words escaped him. If he could just get her here, he could look into her eyes and get a sense if she had feelings for him as well. He began to devise a plan to get Alex to New York.

CHAPTER FIFTEEN

I WAS IN the archive room early the next morning. After an hour of learning the so-called system of organization, I finally located the group of newspapers I had been longing to see. I started reading before the date of my grandfather's death. Several articles alluded to the success of Lyndon and Cook. I had no idea Hayward and his associates had been some of the first developers of downtown Knoxville.

Then I stumbled upon an eye-opener. The newspaper reporter had uncovered a disagreement between the partners. The article described a specific area of lucrative land with an old church and a small cemetery. Mr. Cook was ready to get rid of the run down church and develop the property into a surefire moneymaker. Mr. Lyndon, on the other hand, didn't want to remove the church. He suggested alternative sites as well as drew up plans to utilize the adjacent site without demolishing the church. My grandfather was quoted as basically saying that destroying God's house was unacceptable. He would have no part in doing that. He had a healthy fear of God. Sounded a lot like Granny Olivia. They must have made quite a godly couple!

I continued reading. Just two weeks later, Hayward Lyndon's death was reported. The newspaper story explained the discovery of a prescription bottle of pain medication located on the Mr. Lyndon's desk right next to his lifeless form. Only one pill remained in the bottle. I contemplated the ramifications. A prescription from a doctor would have been required, but Granny had written and Millie had corroborated that he never went to a physician. He also would never have taken any medication. Of course, if Millie was right, Mr. Cook had been connected with many people.

As I was thinking this through, I continued to flip through the newspaper until a photo caught my eye. The man in the photograph looked like the picture of Mr. Cook I had seen in the last article. I studied the picture more closely, willing something to jump out at me. The man was pictured in an advertisement for a pharmacy. The name under the photograph made me gasp—Mr. Cook. He must have been a brother or something. That would explain how the medication could have been obtained. I started to fold up the exhibits and leave, but I felt compelled to keep looking. The headlines of the newspaper one week later after my grandfather's death read, "Giant Sinkhole Ruins Cook's Plans."

Upon reading the rest of the story, I discovered that one day after removing the old church, a giant sinkhole appeared. Mr. Cook should have paid attention to my grandfather's instincts. God surely didn't let the Cooks win or gain from their wrongdoing. I replaced all of the archives, planning to head straight home, but when I spotted the office of Cook's Developing across the street, the car seemed to have a mind of its own.

After parking the car, I sat there trying to decide what I could say after all of these years. This was the place to lay everything to rest. I slid out of the car and squared my shoulders. "This is for you, Granny," I whispered under my breath.

Entering the office, a bright-eyed receptionist greeted me.

"I would like to see Mr. Cook, please."

"Is he expecting you?" The woman gazed at me expectantly.

"Not exactly."

"Well, I'm not sure..." Her eyes darted.

"Just tell him Olivia Lyndon's granddaughter is here." My voice had a firmness I didn't recognize.

"Okay." She stood slowly and motioned for me to stay put.

Within a few minutes a distinguished man emerged from a narrow hallway. He extended his hand to me. "Ms. Lyndon?"

"Yes, Alex Lyndon."

"I'm Kelvin Cook, Jr. Please, come to my office."

I followed him, and he offered me a chair and then plopped into the chair next to me instead of sitting behind his desk.

I turned toward him and made eye contact. "Mr. Cook, I don't want to intrude, but I'm in need of clearing up some things for my Granny Olivia's sake."

"You're not intruding. I always wondered if this day would come."

His words shocked me. "What are you talking about?"

"A day of confession and of possible forgiveness." He hung his head.

"Go on."

"My father was your grandfather's partner. Everything was fine until my father became greedy." He paused for a moment to regain his composure.

This admission seemed to be taking quite a toll on him. "By your demeanor, I suppose my grandmother was correct in saying her husband didn't die from an accidental overdose."

He shook his head. "No, he didn't. It was an overdose, but Mr. Lyndon ingested the medication unknowingly. My uncle obtained the pills."

"He was the pharmacist I saw pictured in the newspaper."

"Yes, my father told me the whole sordid story on his deathbed." Mr. Cook leaned toward me with pleading eyes. "You have to know he was truly repentant."

"Was the true story never told?"

"No, I suppose that's selfish on my part. A story like that could ruin my business, even though I had no part in the crime. I've just kept it to myself all these years. I guess I was afraid. I have a family to support." He looked me in the eyes, and his voice held a desperate tone.

"I know telling the story now would do nothing for anyone. My granny is gone now."

"I know. I'm sorry for your loss. She deserved more." Mr. Cook rubbed the back of his neck.

"Mr. Cook, the only reason I wanted to know the whole truth was for Granny Olivia. I know it sounds strange, but she still wanted to solve this mystery even right before her own death. Now it can be laid to rest."

"I do feel ashamed of my father's actions. I believe the Lord is true to His Word when He talks about sin affecting later generations. The business was never the same after..."

"Would you mind if I told the story in a book I'm writing about Granny's life? I would change names, of course. Granny had her own secrets."

Mr. Cook gave me a quizzical look and then nodded. "You tell the story if you need to." His shoulders slumped as though a boulder was weighing on his back.

I placed my hand on his arm. "Mr. Cook, I hold no malice. Don't carry your father's burden. Let it go."

"Thank you, Ms. Lyndon." He let out a heavy sigh. "The knowledge of this has been like a ticking bomb all these years. I'm glad to finally admit this. If there is anything I can ever do for you, please let me know. I can't make up for what's been done or bring anyone back, but restitution is Biblical."

"Thank you." I held out my hand to him, this time as an act of friendship. He took it with both hands and squeezed.

As I left the office, both of us looked lighter.

"Well, Granny, you were right, and those involved paid dearly for their greed. Guilt is a prison all its own. I know you would have extended the hand of forgiveness, so I did it on your behalf."

CHAPTER SIXTEEN

CHASE SHUFFLED THROUGH some papers on his desk when his assistant buzzed in to announce a call from Mr. Moore. Chase smiled at the mention of the man's name. He and Chase's father had been close friends for years, which was an amazing feat since they were technically rivals. Mr. Moore was also a Christian publisher who began about the same time as the Carson Publishing Company. The two never seemed to have a cross word with one another. They could always be heard encouraging each other. They saw themselves as being on the same team. Trying to make a difference for Jesus Christ.

"Mr. Moore, how are you? "

"Chase, my boy, I am ecstatic!" His baritone echoed through the phone.

"Really? And why is that?" He chuckled.

"I just heard about your dropping Stephanie Radar. I am so proud of you. And, your father would be, too. Trust me, I know."

"Thank you, sir. Those words mean a lot to me. You have no idea. It was difficult to do. I must admit, Satan certainly tempted me with that one. But, I could hear my father's wisdom ringing in my ears. I knew exactly what he would do. Since I still run this business by the Biblical principles he founded it upon, there really was no decision to make."

"Good for you! I've been there. I know what you're going through. I've lost two of my best authors in the last week myself. But, in my opinion, they aren't the best anymore. The principles your father and I established from the beginning still stand. If I can't honor God and uphold His principles, then I'll find another line of work."

"No wonder you and my dad were such good friends. You sound just like him."

Mr. Moore laughed heartily. "Guilty. I miss him so much, but he left his business in good hands. You have proven that this week. Keep it up."

"Mr. Moore, sir, can I ask you a question?"

"Of course, son, anything."

"How do you keep it up? I mean, you have a family, right?"

"Sure do. Just married off the second of three daughters. My baby starts college soon." Pride radiated in his tone. "God has truly blessed me." His voice broke, and he cleared his throat. "Honestly, Chase, there's been crazy times, but you keep your priorities straight and God will honor that."

"Yes, sir."

"God first, then family, then the work He calls you to do. Not always easy, but the Good Lord will lead you."

"How did you know...that your wife was...the one?"

Mr. Moore chuckled. "I couldn't think of anything else after the first time I met her at our church youth group."

"Yeah, I'm there."

"You'll know, son."

"Thanks."

As Chase hung up the phone, he gave God a smile. The Lord knew he needed encouragement, and there it was.

Miss Olivia's book was almost complete. The debut had been set. Now, all Chase needed to do was to set his own plan into action. He just had to get Alex here. He would make it next to impossible to say no to his invitation this time.

CHAPTER SEVENTEEN

ON MONDAY MORNING I was startled by a knock at the door.

"Special delivery for Alex Lyndon."

"That's me."

The man shoved a flat device toward me. "Sign here, please."

"Thank you."

Special delivery? I closed the door and tore into the envelope.

Dear Alex,

Enclosed is a plane ticket and confirmation for a hotel room. Please say yes. Come to New York. We will debut your grandmother's book with a special party. Be my date?

Love, Chase

I scanned the dates on the tickets. Friday. Did I dare? I would so love to be there for this last book debut. The thought of being near Chase again sent a tingling feeling all the way to my toes. He had signed the note with *love*. What kind of love did he mean? I wished for the "happily ever after" from Granny Olivia's books. Her stories ended with right always winning, and the guy and girl together. Did that still happen in real life or was I only dreaming?

Early that evening my cell phone buzzed.

"Did you get it?" Excitement rang in Chase's voice.

"Yes."

"Well? You're not gonna turn me down are you? I have my best puppy dog eyes right now."

I laughed because I could imagine those eyes.

"Okay."

"Great! I'll be there to meet your plane Friday. I can't wait for you to get here."

His excitement poured through the phone, increasing mine.

By the time the call ended, I was sure this week would be long due to my anticipation.

To prepare, I first needed a new dress. A party in New York for the debut of a book as popular as Granny's would be fancier than the church dresses I owned. It took two days of morning shopping until I finally discovered something. A simple yet elegant black dress that the sales lady said flattered me. I had never been able to ignore the price tag and just buy something for myself. The inheritance money allowed me to splurge a bit, though it was hard not to shop with my normal frugalness. I also purchased some slacks and fall sweaters. I supposed New York would be cooler right now than East Tennessee. I also procured a nice satchel to carry my journals and writing paraphernalia. There was no way I could leave that at home for the long weekend. It was difficult to let it go at times. I was nearing completion on Granny's story, and the other fiction was coming along.

The clothes and accessories might make me appear to fit in there in New York, but I would know the truth. But, what if? Could a nobody like me pull this off? Cinderella for a weekend. I had barely been outside the county, much less outside of the state of Tennessee.

I had done very little traveling in my life—but then again, there was a sense of adventure to this trip. My stomach was tied in knots. Friday morning arrived sunny and cool. I hauled my luggage to the front walk just as the van pulled up to take me to the airport. I fidgeted the whole ride there. I bounded through the terminal, checked my suitcases, and awaited the flight's call. Finally the call came to board the plane. I located my seat, settled in, and noted the older woman to my right and the younger one to my left. I greeted each and proceeded to pull out another of Granny's books. I was still reading some of her work, taking note of her technique and writing, using her example.

As soon as I opened the book, the woman on my right nudged my arm. "Ooo, I read that one last year. That's a good one. I've read everything Alexa Livingston has ever written."

The woman on the other side of me joined in. "Me, too! I just love her writing. I've been waiting for the last book in this latest series. It seems like forever." She leaned forward.

"Me, too. I just have to find out what happens to Chance and Dominique."

My grin stretched from one of my ears to the other. These two women were about to get their wish.

"So, are you enjoying them?" the older woman said.

"Oh, yes. I really just discovered these books recently, so I've been reading to catch up."

The younger woman leaned around me to look at the other. "You know, I wonder what kind of series Alexa will write next."

"Honey, it'll be hard to top this one."

A sadness cinched my chest. There would be no other series from Alexa Livingston. These two women talked as if they knew her personally. I was sure they felt as if they did through her many books. I had been grieved to lose my granny, but I suddenly realized there were many others who would grieve her loss, too. Each woman returned to reading or sleeping, so I returned to my book. Upon arrival, I thanked the ladies for their advice about the books. On the inside, I was thankful to hear from Granny's fans. They adored her and didn't really know who she was.

Stepping through the gate, my eyes caught sight of Chase and a shiver ran through my body. He ran toward me and wrapped me in a warm embrace that felt like home.

"That was a nice welcome."

"There's more where that came from. "

I raised my eyebrows in response.

When we had retrieved and stowed all of my luggage in Chase's car, we headed toward my hotel.

"I want to take you to dinner tonight. Casual. The fancy stuff is tomorrow night. I'm so excited for you to be here at the book debut. We have other authors coming." His words tumbled out quickly.

A knot tightened in my stomach. Where did I fit in all this? Did he expect me to reveal who I was or to say something? He must have read my mind because he continued.

"And, don't feel pressured. I won't reveal your identity unless you want me to." He glanced at me out of the corner of his eye. "I want you to be able to enjoy the moment with no paparazzi hounding you."

I let out a breath. "Thanks. I'm not sure I'm cut out to say anything. In fact, I had the opportunity on the plane ride here, but didn't take it. I didn't want it."

Chase looked at me rather confused. I proceeded to tell him about the two women on the airplane.

"There are many people all over the country who have that same sentiment, and they will be thrilled about this last book just like those two women."

"What are you going to say about Granny Olivia?"

"I'm not going to reveal everything, because that would make it much too easy to track her down and her house and you." His expression changed momentarily to sad. "I am going to announce she has passed, so this last book is precious. The end of the story in many ways."

"I realized sitting on the plane, listening to those two ladies, that you would definitely have to at least tell of her passing. They are already trying to figure out what she'll write next." My voice cracked.

Chase put his hand over mine. "Are you okay?"

"Yes, all of this is so surreal, but the fact remains, Granny's gone."

"I know." His voice trailed off.

Chase checked me in at the hotel and escorted me to my room with a promise to be back for me at five. I plopped onto the bed with a heavy sigh. I was really here. I grabbed the journal containing Granny's story and began to add the sentiments I had learned from her fans on the plane.

Chase showed up right on time, looking quite appealing in a casual blazer and jeans. He escorted me to a seat in a quaint little café. Being with him was comfortable and yet exciting all at once. Upon ordering our food, he covered my hand with his and looked me in the eyes. I was having trouble breathing normal being near him again.

"Let me give you a run-down on tomorrow's schedule." His eyes danced, and he chattered on at a rapid pace. I couldn't help but hope that his enthusiasm wasn't only due to the book debut. "I'll pick you up for breakfast, and then we'll whisk over to the publishing company so I can give you a tour and show you off." He grinned and winked. "Then, we'll have a couple of hours to see some of the sights and then back to the hotel to get ready for the big evening." He sipped his soda and clicked his lips. "How does that sound?"

"Wonderful."

I could hardly sleep that night after Chase walked me to my hotel door. But, gladly, I had my journals, which I wrote in feverishly. Until almost two in the morning.

I was much too eager to sleep in, so by the time Chase knocked on the door, I was ready to dive into our itinerary.

"Wow, you're up and at it." Chase's brows rose.

"I don't want to miss anything." I especially didn't want to miss out on a second being with Chase.

After breakfast, I followed Chase into a tall building and onto a shiny elevator.

"Now, you can see where all the publishing magic happens." His eyes shone like a kid at Christmas. The elevator doors opened. The wall directly outside bore large golden letters spelling out Carson Publishing Company. Chase grabbed my hand and guided me to the right. He waved to a receptionist.

"Hey, Glenna."

She nodded. "Mr. Carson."

Chase stopped at a set of double doors at the end of the hall. To the left another woman sat at an L-shaped desk. Her head popped up.

"Alex, this is my assistant, Carol. This is Alex Lyndon."

Carol crossed the distance between us and took my other hand. "Nice to meet you."

"Yes, it's nice to meet you, too," I said. Carol looked to Chase as if awaiting more of an explanation.

"I'm giving her the grand tour." He opened one of the double doors, pulled me inside, and closed the doors behind us."

"Here is my office. I still have a hard time calling it that because it was my father's."

I stood motionless, taking in my surroundings.

The room was huge, accommodating a large wooden desk as the focal point. An oval table with five chairs stood in one corner. A couch with matching chairs flanked the wall across from the desk. Although, the wall was not a solid wall, it was a large window. The glass panels reached ceiling to floor and displayed the skyline of New York. It resembled something from a movie.

I walked toward the large window. "Wow, what a view!"

"I suppose if you like city skylines. I think that's one of the reasons I continued to travel to your granny's house. Now that's a view. Those beautiful mountains as a backdrop to everything. The pace was much more to my liking as well. Slower was refreshing."

"Really? I would've thought this would be what you were used to." I indicated the view as well as the expansive office.

"We do what we must sometimes. There was no one else to step in when my father died. I do love the work, as I've said before. I enjoy providing Christian books that impact people's lives."

"But?"

"But, there are times, I don't think I fit here."

My breath caught. He didn't feel like he fit in New York. Had he really said that?

"Publishing and editing are all I know."

I giggled. "Sorry, I have to admit, my idea of a publisher was some old man with a cigar giving orders to his printers. I don't know why."

"Nope, just little ol' me. My father did a good job starting this company and getting people who are good at what they do. It practically runs itself."

I tilted my head and gave him a look of disbelief. "I'm sure you're being modest, but humbleness is an attractive quality." I said that last part before I thought of how it would sound. Of course, it was what I was thinking and the truth.

Chase gave me a sly look. "If you find humbleness attractive, I'll make sure I try to have some."

Some heat rose to my cheeks. I needed to work on not being so honest and transparent or my cheeks were going to stay permanently a nice shade of red.

After our tour of Carson Publishing Company, we strolled down the street. Chase pointed out different buildings and sights I had heard of but never seen in person. The sidewalks were fairly busy, so he reached for my hand and held it during the tour. His hand felt so natural holding to mine. I was hesitant to allow myself to fully enjoy these moments. In just two short days, I would fly back to Greeneville. My life was there now. I wasn't sure of God's exact plans for me, but I believed I was where I was supposed to be right now. Chase was here carrying on his father's work, a worthwhile legacy. As much as I would like to see the two of us together, it was a long way between here and Tennessee.

By the time he dropped me at the hotel after sightseeing, I was tired. I was glad to find I could fit in a nap before I needed to get ready for the debut. I awoke with another thought about the story I was composing, so I reached for the journal and added it in.

CHAPTER EIGHTEEN

I HAD ALMOST completed my hair and makeup routine when Chase knocked. As I opened the door, his eyes bulged.

"You look beautiful."

"Thank you. You look dashing yourself." I peeled my eyes away from his sleek black tux. "I'm just about ready. I only need to put on the finishing touches."

"I'm a bit early. Sorry. I guess I'm excited."

No one would have to guess. His excitement was evident. His blue eyes danced. I stepped back into the bathroom for a little more hairspray and a touch of lip gloss. I raised my voice so Chase could hear me in the other room.

"I'm excited, too. This will be a great night."

I emerged from the bathroom to find Chase perched on the side of the bed with two of my journals in his hands. I froze.

He held the books up. "These aren't your grandmother's, are they?"

I shook my head and swallowed at the lump that suddenly rose in my throat. "No."

He rose from the bed. "These are good. The story of your grandmother's life would be the absolute grandest finale to her writing career. And, this." He held up one of the red journals containing the fiction I had been working on. "This is amazing. You must have gotten that writing gene from your granny after all."

"Do you really think so? You're not just saying that?" I bit at my thumbnail.

"No, I'm not just saying that. These are incredible." He dropped the books on the bed and took me in his arms. His face was mere centimeters from mine. "I think you might have found your calling. Will you let me take them to read?"

"Oh, I don't know." My stomach tightened. The thought of someone reading my thoughts made me feel so vulnerable. I had written in journals all my life, but never had I given them over to another person to read through. My heart and soul were in those books. But, if there was anyone I was close enough to, it would be Chase. "Okay, you can read them."

"Thanks. Now, let's go enjoy the party."

I smiled. Before he released me, he pulled me into a kiss and an excited spark shot through me.

As we stepped from the car, Chase handed his key to the valet. He joined me on the sidewalk where I was admiring the fancy hotel entrance. He offered his arm, and I slid my hand through, resting it on his forearm. He patted my hand and gazed into my eyes. "Ready." I took a deep breath, let it out, and nodded. Walking into the hotel, I felt like a princess attending her first ball.

At first sight of the banquet hall, I gasped, and my eyes clouded with tears. "It's beautiful." Round tables were decked with white cloths and floral centerpieces. Two giant posters of Granny Olivia's book cover flanked a small raised podium.

"Mr. Carson," a female voice said. I tore my gaze from the décor and looked into the eyes of a tall slender blonde in a long green dress. Her brows rose.

"Lisa, this is Miss Lyndon. Lisa is one of our acquisition editors."

Lisa smiled, extended her hand, and we shook. When she disappeared into the growing crowd, Chase leaned close to my ear and whispered. "I thought it safer to introduce you as Miss Lyndon since Alex and Alexa are so similar." I nodded. I appreciated his forethought and consideration. As Chase led me through the minglers to the front table, he introduced me to other attendees. I recognized some of the names as other Christian authors. I was honored and thrilled to be in their company.

"Here's where we'll be." He gestured toward a table at the front. He took my hand and pulled gently. "You have to meet my mother."

My stomach fluttered. As we neared the table, a woman stood, looking regal in a long red dress. Her gray-white hair was shoulder length, coifed to perfection. She smiled as she noticed our approach.

"Alex, this is my mother, Angela Carson. Mom, this is Alex Lyndon."

I extended my hand, but Mrs. Carson bypassed it and pulled me into an embrace. She pulled back and gazed into my eyes. "It's so wonderful to meet you."

"The pleasure is mine, Mrs. Carson." I could see where Chase had gotten his beautiful blue eyes.

"Come, sit here."

"Thank you."

Chase made his way to the podium and asked everyone to take their seats. After about fifteen minutes, he addressed the crowd.

"I want to thank all of you who are in attendance this evening to launch a very special book." Chase's voice broke, and he looked down. He cleared his throat and lifted his head again. "I'm sorry for the emotions, but this book launch will be quite different from any you may have attended before." He gripped the sides of the podium. "Alexa Livingston has always embodied the very mission of Carson Publishing Company. It was never about her, but all for God's glory. This is why Ms. Livingston never revealed her identity. She wrote for her precious readers, not for fame or money." Chase paused.

My bottom lip began to quiver.

Chase stole a quick glance my way and then looked back across the audience. He gestured toward the book cover. "This book is the last in a series, and Alexa Livingston's last."

A concerted gasp emitted from the crowd.

"Mrs. Livingston surely heard well done when she entered heaven."

Several people sniffed and then fumbled for tissues to catch tears.

I wished that Granny Olivia could just have a glimpse of this. All these people she had touched. On second thought, I chuckled at that wish. As grand as this banquet was, I knew she had to be enjoying a much grander feast in Heaven. That most certainly paled compared to our feeble attempts to honor her.

Chase completed his remarks and joined his mother and me for the dinner. The food was delicious, and the conversation was savory as well.

Chase escorted me to my hotel room door after the festivities, unlocking and opening it for me. We stepped inside. I looked into his eyes. "This evening was so wonderful. Thank you for bringing me here to share in it."

Chase's hands rested on my waist, and he pulled me near. "I wouldn't have had it any other way." He touched my cheek with his hand. "I liked having you on my arm and by my side." He leaned near, and our lips met. My whole body felt electrified, tingling from head to toe. His warm lips lingered on mine, and his arms tugged me closer. A rush of warmth spread through me, and I relaxed in his arms. Suddenly, he stopped the kiss and leaned his head back. I opened my eyes to find him looking at me. His mouth broke into a grin. "I better go before I..." He breathed in and let the air out slowly.

Slipping by me, he scooped up the journals I had promised he could read.

"I'll see you in the morning, not too early." He kissed my cheek lightly and met my eyes when he pulled back. He let out a low moan and backed toward the door.

"Goodnight."

"Night, Chase."

I leaned my back on the closed door, missing him already. His honorable restraint made Chase Carson even more attractive.

CHASE HURRIED BACK to his apartment, barely pausing to shuck his tuxedo. Halfway through Alex's fiction story, he punched the number for Lisa, one of his acquisitions editors.

"Chase?" A panic rang in her voice. "It's got to be—"

"Lisa, sorry I'm calling so late. I thought you'd probably still be up after the debut."

"Yeah. What's wrong?"

"Nothing's wrong. Something's really right. Or, that is, someone."

"Chase, are you okay? Does this have anything to do with the woman I saw on your arm tonight?"

"Everything to do with her."

"Miss Lyndon, right?"

"Right. Alex. Could you meet me for coffee?"

"Now?"

"Yes."

Chase raced to the coffee house with Alex's journals in hand. When Lisa arrived, he offered her a cup of her favorite java. She sipped and then leveled her eyes at him.

He pushed the journals across the table. "Skim a few pages of these."

She opened the top book. As she turned the first page, she leaned closer with interest. After a few more pages, she looked up, mouth agape. "Who is this?"

Chase grinned.

Lisa's eyes widened and she bent her head across the table and lowered her voice. "Alex? Your Alex?"

Chase nodded.

"Where did she learn...?" She waved the journals.

"Let's just say she's sat under a master for years."

Lisa sat back, folding her arms. "Can we sign her?"

"I'll ask her."

On the way back to his apartment, he called his mother.

"Mom, I'm sorry it's so late. I was hoping you might still be awake."

"It just so happens I am still up. I felt compelled to pray."

Chase chuckled. "I think I know why. I believe God's leading me to make some changes."

EARLY THE NEXT morning, there was a banging on my hotel door. I moaned and proceeded to peer through the peep hole. It was Chase. I looked down at my mussed appearance. Quite different from the polished look of last night. He knocked again. I cracked the door. "What's wrong?" my voice squeaked out.

He pushed open the door and barged in. "Nothing is wrong. Everything is right."

"What?"

"Good morning, by the way." He put his arm briefly around my waist and kissed my forehead. Then he pulled out the desk chair and plopped into it. "We need to talk."

My stomach tightened. What was this all about?

"I have hardly slept."

He did appear disheveled as well. "Were you ill?" I sat on the edge of the bed.

He turned until his knees were against mine. "No, I'm not ill. Far from it. Alex, these are terrific." He held up my journals.

"Thank you. I'm flattered you would find them terrific."

"I showed them to Lisa, the acquisitions editor at Carson you met, and she is ready to sign you today."

I felt my eyes widen. "What? Publish my stuff?"

"Yes. What do you say? Will you become one of Carson's up and coming authors?"

"I don't know what to say." I stood and paced for a moment, letting the shock wear off. "If I do this I want to stay anonymous, like Granny Olivia did. I'm just a small town girl."

"I can arrange that." He nodded.

I smiled. "I can't believe this." I paced a small path in front of him, rubbing my hands down my face. "You're not just being nice?"

"No. Alex, your writing is amazing."

I bit my lip and stared into his eyes.

Chase caught my hand and stopped me. "If you're going to stay anonymous, we'll have to come up with a pen name for you." He stroked his chin. "How about your middle name and maiden name just like your grandmother?—Michelle Lyndon."

"I can't do that. I took my maiden name back after the divorce. Lyndon is my name."

Chase rose to his feet and embraced me. "Not if I give you a married name."

My pulse quickened. Could he really mean what I thought he meant?

"Will you marry me? Will you become a Carson?"

"Oh, Chase, I do love you and would love to be your wife, but I'm not sure how well I'd fit in around here." My insides trembled.

"You don't have to. I much prefer the incognito life back in Tennessee at your house. That is, if you'll have me? I mean, I need to be there to look out for my new author personally, just like I did for Miss Olivia. I don't do that for just anybody, you know."

I flung my arms around his neck. "Yes, yes!"

CHAPTER NINETEEN

A WEDDING IN Granny Olivia's back yard seemed the perfect place. Granny's pastor would do the honors, and all of the people whom she had touched were there to wish us well. I found a white lacy tea-length dress that resembled the pictures of Granny Olivia's wedding dress.

Millie insisted on providing fresh flowers from her yard for a bouquet. She handed them to me and smiled approvingly. "Your Granny Olivia would be so happy for you." Her eyes misted over, and she diverted them from me.

"Thank you, Millie." I gave her a half hug.

I stood alone in the kitchen, watching out the door for my cue.

"Alex, dear?" I turned to find Chase's mother.

"Mrs. Carson."

She grasped my hand and squeezed.

"It's Mom from now on."

My eyes blurred with tears, and the lump of emotion in my throat prohibited me from speaking. I nodded.

"I'm so happy for you and my son. I've prayed for you since he was just a little boy."

I finally managed to squeak out a thank you.

"I better get out there." She moved toward the door.

I touched her arm. "Wait." She turned around. "Will you walk with me?"

Her eyes widened.

I shrugged one shoulder. "I don't have any family left to walk me to the altar."

She caressed my cheek with the back of her hand. "Oh, precious child, you have a family."

She offered her hand, and I took it.

We walked hand-in-hand across the yard. I could barely see my handsome groom for the tears.

After Chase kissed me and we were pronounced man and wife, I admitted something to him.

"I wish Granny Olivia was here to share this day with us."

"For some reason, I think she knows. I know it is God who makes the plans for our lives, but I just feel like she helped Him author this happily ever after."

I had to agree.

I thanked God for this happy ending and for giving me Granny Olivia, whose godly influence taught me to find my happily ever after.

ABOUT THE AUTHOR

Paula Mowery is a published author, acquisitions editor, and speaker. Her first two published works were *The Blessing Seer* and *Be The Blessing* from Pelican Book Group. Both are women's fiction, and their themes have been the topics of speaking engagements. In November of 2013, her first romance released in the anthology, *Brave New Century*, from Prism Book Group. *Legacy and Love* is her first solo romance. Reviewers of her writing characterize it as "thundering with emotion." Her articles have appeared in *Woman's World*, *The Christian Online Magazine*, and the multi-author devotional blog, *Full Flavored Living*.

As an acquisitions editor for Prism Book Group, Paula particularly looks for romance stories with Christian values at its core. She's especially attracted to those manuscripts that leave the reader mulling over the story long after turning the last page.

Having been an avid reader of Christian fiction, she now puts that love to use by writing book reviews. She is a member of ACFW and is on the author interview team.

Paula is a pastor's wife and mom to a first year college student. She homeschooled her daughter through all twelve years, and they both lived to tell about it. Before educating her daughter at home, she was an English teacher in public school.

You can follow Paula at www.facebook.com/pages/Paula-Mowery/175869562589187. Learn more about Paula at her blog at www.paulamowery.blogspot.com or enjoy her monthly columns on www.christianonlinemagazine.com.

Thank you for your Prism Book Group purchase! Visit our website to enjoy free reads, great deals, and entertaining, wholesome fiction!

http://www.prismbookgroup.com